You're Invited to a

CREEPOVER™

No Trick-or-Treating!

Superscary Superspecial

written by P. J. Night

SIMON SPOTLIGHT
New York London Toronto Sydney New Delhi

SIMON SPOTLIGHT
An imprint of Simon & Schuster Children's Publishing Division
1230 Avenue of the Americas, New York, New York 10020

Text by Ellie O'Ryan
For information about special discounts for bulk purchases, please contact Simon & Schuster Special Sales at 1-866-506-1949 or business@simonandschuster.com.
Manufactured in the United States of America 0712 OFF
First Edition 10 9 8 7 6 5 4 3 2 1
ISBN 978-1-4424-5053-0
ISBN 978-1-4424-5054-7 (eBook)
Library of Congress Catalog Card Number 2012933329

CHAPTER 1

Click.

Ashley blinked in the sudden brightness. The bare lightbulb overhead swung from a rusty chain, casting shadows all over her new bedroom. She squinted in the harsh light, but it was the best she could do until she unpacked the little purple lamp that had sat on her bedside table for as long as she could remember.

Besides, she told herself, glancing from the boxes scattered over the pocked floor to the four-foot crack running down the wall, *it's not like this room could look any worse.*

Ashley sighed, for the thousandth time, as she remembered her old bedroom back in Atlanta. It was perfect in every way, from the pale-aqua paint on the walls to the window seat that overlooked the alley, a quiet place in a bustling city. But that was all gone now; Ashley knew she'd probably never see her room again. Maybe, right this very minute, somebody else was sitting in her old room, starting to unpack a bunch of boxes.

Lucky, Ashley thought, flopping back on her bare mattress and staring at the stain-spotted ceiling. She knew she should put the sheets on her bed, but she just didn't feel like doing anything.

There was a knock at the door. Ashley could tell from the four strong raps that it was her mother. *Maybe if I ignore her, she'll go away,* Ashley thought.

The knock came again, and then the door creaked open.

"Hey, Pumpkin!" Mrs. McDowell called out in a cheerful voice. "How's it going in here? Want some help?"

Ashley shrugged and rolled over on the bed so that she was facing the window. It was getting dark outside—a deeper darkness than she was used to. It never felt dark in Atlanta, not really dark, not with all the streetlights and headlights and towering buildings whose windows glowed all night long. But this far out in the country, light was harder to come by once the sun went down.

The bed creaked as Mrs. McDowell sat behind Ashley

and started rubbing her back. Ashley inched away. She knew she was probably hurting her mom's feelings, but it was hard to care. After all, it wasn't like her mom and dad had cared about *her* feelings when they'd decided to sell their apartment and buy this rundown farm out in the middle of nowhere.

"This is going to be a really great thing, Ashley," Mrs. McDowell said yet again. "Just try to have faith, okay? I know change is hard and stressful and scary—"

"Scary? Um, no. I'm not *scared*. I'm *bored*. I hate it here."

"You hate it here?" Mrs. McDowell said. "Pumpkin, we've only been in Heaton Corners for, oh, five hours or so. All I ask is that you give it a chance. You know Dad and I wouldn't make a decision this big if we didn't think it was the best thing for everyone."

"But you didn't even *ask* me," Ashley replied, blinking back tears. "I don't *want* to live on a smelly farm, Mom. I miss Atlanta so much."

Mrs. McDowell sighed. "We really regret not leaving the city before Maya went to college," she said in a quiet voice. "We don't want to make the same mistake with you. Maya spent her whole childhood cooped up in that apartment—"

"Yeah, and she loved it!" Ashley interrupted. "And so did I!"

"Can you try to think of it as an adventure?" Mrs. McDowell asked, and there was something so vulnerable in her voice that Ashley finally sat up and looked at her. "You know there's something really exciting about a fresh start, going to a whole new school and meeting all kinds of new people! And we'll have the homestead up and running before you know it—the chicks will arrive in a few days; won't that be fun? Little fluffy baby chickens? And next spring we'll get a cow!"

Ashley started to laugh. It was such a ridiculous thing to say—"we'll get a cow!"—that she couldn't help herself. And she couldn't miss the relief that flooded her mom's eyes.

"And maybe," Ashley said, wishing that she wasn't giving in so easily but saying it anyway, "we can fix that horrible crack over there? It looks like the wall got struck by lightning."

Mrs. McDowell smiled as she patted Ashley's knee. "Of course. I'll have Dad come take a look—we can probably patch that crack by the end of the week. And then we'll get the walls primed for painting. Have you thought about what color you want? Maybe a nice, sunny yellow?"

"Aqua," Ashley said firmly. "Just like my old room."

"All right," Mrs. McDowell said. "Whatever you want. Listen, Dad went to get pizza; I think he'll be back in an hour or so."

"That long?" Ashley asked. "To grab pizza?"

"Well, it turns out there's no pizza place in Heaton Corners," Mrs. McDowell said, sighing. "So he had to drive all the way to Walthrop."

Ashley sneered. "Seriously. What kind of town doesn't have a pizza place? Heaton Corners is the worst. The *worst.*"

"No, no, it's not so bad," Mrs. McDowell said. "We'll learn to make our *own* pizza! And after we get the vegetable garden going next summer, we'll even make our own sauce! With our own tomatoes!"

Yeah. Great, Ashley thought. *Or, you know, we could get a pizza from Bernini's in, like, ten minutes. If we still lived in Atlanta.*

"So, come down when you can, and help me find the plates," Mrs. McDowell said as she stood up. On her way out, she paused by the door. "Oh, Ashley? Did I see your bike out back?"

"Yeah, probably."

"Go out and put it in the barn, okay?"

"Why?" Ashley argued. "We're in the middle of nowhere, remember? Nobody's going to steal it."

"Probably not," Mrs. McDowell replied. Then she pointed at the window. "But it looks like it's going to rain tonight. You see those thunderheads gathering? So go ahead and get your bike in the barn so it doesn't rust. Thanks, Pumpkin."

Ashley sighed heavily as her mom left. Then she halfheartedly started rummaging through one of the boxes on the floor. She didn't exactly feel like unpacking, but she definitely didn't feel like rushing outside to put away her bike just because her mom said so.

Of course, there was no way for Ashley to know that that particular carton held her Memory Box, a dark-purple shoebox that was crammed with photos, cards, and funny notes from her best friends in Atlanta. Just seeing Nora's and Lucy's handwriting made Ashley feel homesick. By the time she'd finished rereading every single note, it was pitch-black outside.

And her mom was shouting from the kitchen.

"Ashley! Your bike! And I'm going to need your help in here!"

Ashley shoved the Memory Box under her bed and went downstairs, walking right past the kitchen without saying a word to her mom. Her flip-flops were near the back door, where she'd kicked them off after the movers had left. One look out the window told Ashley that she would need a flashlight to find the barn. Luckily, there was a flashlight hanging right next to the door. Ashley guessed that the last people who'd lived here had found themselves in the same situation.

She switched on the flashlight and stepped outside. Its bright-yellow beam pierced through the night sky, then quickly faded to a dull orange. Ashley shook the flashlight and smacked it against her palm until it glowed a little brighter.

Typical, she thought. *I bet the batteries will die as soon as I get into the barn.*

The thought made Ashley walk a little faster as she wheeled her bike through the overgrown goldenrod toward the barn. It hadn't started raining yet, but the weeds were damp with evening dew, and she shivered as they slapped against her bare legs. And her toes were *freezing*. Ashley hated to admit it, but her mom was right: Sandal season was *definitely* over.

As Ashley walked, she remembered what her mom had said about Maya: "We really regret not leaving the city before Maya went to college." *It just shows how clueless my parents are,* Ashley thought. Her big sister had *never* wanted to live in the country. That's why she'd decided to go to college in Chicago. It had been a little more than a month since Maya had moved into her dorm, and Ashley missed her every day. Talking on the phone or chatting online just wasn't the same. And Chicago felt so far away to Ashley. It wasn't even in the same state. It wasn't even in the same time zone!

Just before Ashley reached the barn, the flashlight died, but in a stroke of luck the clouds parted for a moment, letting through enough moonlight that she could lift the heavy iron latch on the barn door. The only sound Ashley could hear was the soft *squeeeeeeak* of the bike's gears as she pushed it into the barn.

The air in the barn was dry and dusty; it smelled of caked dirt and hay. The moment Ashley stepped in from the barn door, it slammed shut with such a loud bang that she jumped. Without even the weak beam of the flashlight to guide her steps, Ashley was plunged into pitch-black darkness. She stretched her arm out as far as it would reach, until her fingers grazed the rough, unfinished wood of the barn wall. Then she took one careful step at a time until she found a spot to leave her bike. Ashley leaned it against the wall and turned to leave.

C-r-r-r-r-unch.

She froze.

What, Ashley thought as her heart started to pound, *did I just step on?*

There was something leathery, something papery, something scaly, something she couldn't quite place—flicking against her bare skin. Was it slithering over her feet, twining around her ankles? Or was that just her imagination?

Had it been *waiting* for someone to set foot inside this old, abandoned barn?

Stop it, Ashley told herself firmly. She was a city girl. She was not the kind of person who freaked out over every little thing. With a surge of confidence, she hit the flashlight against her palm again.

Thwak. Thwak. Thwak.

Suddenly a pale beam flashed across the barn. The flashlight was working again, for a minute, at least.

Ashley pointed the flashlight at her feet. It took a moment—longer, probably—for her to realize what she was standing in; some part of her brain couldn't, *wouldn't* accept it. There were so many that she couldn't count them, especially because of the way they wriggled—

Wait. *Were* they moving? Or was that just the effect of her clumsy feet as she stumbled, trying to escape?

Either way, Ashley didn't stick around to find out. She screamed—she couldn't help it—as the weak light from the flashlight died again. Ashley rushed out of the barn, still screaming, and her screams echoed across the farm, almost as if they were ricocheting off the heavy clouds that were crowding the sky once more.

She was so preoccupied by the memory of those slithery *things* on her feet, and so distracted by the utter darkness, that she didn't see the tall figure step out from the shadows . . .

Until a pair of strong hands grabbed her shoulders and held on tight!

CHAPTER 2

Ashley screamed so loudly that her whole body shuddered from the effort. She twisted away violently, flailing her arms, until she recognized the voice of the person holding her.

"Ashley! Ashley! Stop, Ashley, what's wrong?"

"Dad!" she cried. An overwhelming feeling of relief flooded through her veins, but it was soon replaced by embarrassment. "When did you—"

"I just got back from Walthrop," Mr. McDowell replied. He pointed at the pizza box he had dropped on the ground. "Ashley, what happened? I got out of the truck and heard you screaming—"

"Oh," Ashley said. "I was, um, in the barn and I stepped in, I don't know, like, a nest of—*snakes* or something."

"A nest of snakes?" Mr. McDowell repeated. "What kind?"

"I don't know," Ashley replied, staring at the ground. "I didn't exactly stick around to find out. And, besides, the flashlight went dead."

"I want to take a look at that nest," Mr. McDowell said. He switched on the superbright LCD penlight on his key chain. "Want to come with me?"

"That's okay," Ashley said at once. "I think I've spent enough time in the barn tonight. Thanks anyway."

Mr. McDowell stooped down to pick up the pizza box. "Would you take the pizza inside?" he said. "I'll be back in a minute."

Ashley watched her dad's silhouette move away into the darkness. "Dad, wait," she said, panic creeping into her voice. "Just—just leave it. You can go look at the snakes tomorrow, okay? Please?"

She heard him chuckle in the darkness. "I'll be careful," he told her.

Ashley didn't reply as she walked up to the house. She didn't see the point of poking around in the barn when it was pitch-black outside.

"Oh, is that the pizza?" Mrs. McDowell asked as

Ashley walked into the kitchen. "Finally! I'm starving! Where's your dad?"

"In the barn," Ashley said.

"The barn?" Mrs. McDowell sounded puzzled. "Why? It's time to eat."

Ashley shrugged. She didn't feel like getting into it. "Here. This flashlight needs new batteries."

"Okay. Just put it on the counter, and I'll find some later."

Ashley set the flashlight next to the pizza box and peeked inside it. She had to admit that the pizza, smothered in vegetables and crisp pepperoni, looked pretty good—so good that she broke off a piece of the crust and started nibbling it. Then she made a face. "It's kind of cold," she pointed out.

"Ashley, you know I hate it when you start eating right out of the box." Mrs. McDowell sighed. "You'll have to microwave your piece if it bothers you."

Ugh, rubbery pizza, Ashley thought. But she didn't say anything, because at that moment her dad walked through the back door.

"I found your snake pit, Ashley," he said as he casually tossed something at her feet.

Ashley jumped back and shrieked before she could stop herself.

"What is *that*?" Mrs. McDowell asked with disgust dripping from her voice. "And why is it in my house?"

"It's a snake skin," Mr. McDowell explained. "I thought Ash'd be relieved to know that she only stumbled through a pile of snake *skins*—not real snakes."

Ashley shuddered. "Ugh, gross," she said defensively. "And it was dark, and I felt them, like, flicking against my bare feet! How was I supposed to know they weren't alive?"

Ashley's parents exchanged a smile, and she rolled her eyes. She wished they would start treating her like an adult—instead of some little pet who made them laugh.

"Honey, we're living on a farm now," Mrs. McDowell reminded Ashley—as if she could forget. "If you're going outside, you need to wear your boots—or at least your sneakers."

"Especially when you go to the barn," Mr. McDowell added. "Nobody's lived here for at least five years. There could be rusty nails, brown recluse spiders—"

"Okay, okay, I get it," Ashley cut him off. "Can we please eat now?"

"Yes. Just as soon as your dad takes that thing outside," Mrs. McDowell said firmly.

"Weird, though, isn't it?" Mr. McDowell said as he picked up the snake skin. "Snakes don't molt in a nest. So this pile must've been collected by somebody. And it must've taken a long time to find so many snake skins."

Mrs. McDowell waved her hand dismissively and took the pizza box out to the dining room table. "Time to stop talking about snakes and start eating. Don't forget to wash your hands before you come to the table, you two."

As Ashley washed her hands at the deep, stained sink in the kitchen, she glanced out the window. She could see a few fallen leaves swoop by on a gust of wind, and she wished—for the thousandth time—that they could move back to the city.

But Ashley knew better than to even ask.

"Just drop me off at the corner," Ashley said the next morning. "I can walk the rest of the way. You don't have to drop me off right in front."

"But, honey, it looks like there's a carpool line over

there," Mrs. McDowell said. "Wouldn't you rather—"

"No," Ashley replied. She'd already noticed how her parents' brand-new truck stood out; it was candy-apple red, with such shiny paint that it seemed to glitter in the sunlight. The other trucks around town looked like they'd been on the road for twenty years, with chipped paint, rusty bumpers, and more than a few dents. It was hard enough starting school in the first week of October after everyone had settled into a routine; Ashley didn't want to stand out any more than she had to today, on her first day of school in Heaton Corners.

"Have a great day, Pumpkin!" Mrs. McDowell chirped as she pulled over to the corner. "You want me to pick you up this afternoon?"

"No, thanks," Ashley said firmly. "I can walk."

"You sure?" Mrs. McDowell asked as worry flickered across her face. "Do you remember the—"

"Straight down Rural Route 12, turn left onto the side road that runs next to Perseverance Creek, then right onto Rural Route 13. I remember," Ashley interrupted.

"Okay. I can't wait to hear all about your first day at your new school!" her mom said with a big smile.

Ashley smiled back—or tried to, at least—and

then she climbed out of the truck.

The first thing Ashley noticed was how *small* Heaton Corners Junior/Senior High was; it was kind of hard to believe that seven different grades of students all attended school in the same building. The school was two stories tall, built of faded orange bricks that had been weathered from decades of exposure to the elements. The small windows had been washed recently; they sparkled in the morning light. A bell tower perched on top of the slate-gray roof.

The second thing Ashley noticed was the group of kids staring at her. She looked straight ahead, trying to pretend that she hadn't seen them.

"Nice truck," one of the guys called out. He was definitely in high school.

"Uh, thanks," Ashley replied.

Just then Mrs. McDowell pulled a U-turn and honked the horn as she drove past Ashley on her way back to the farm. Ashley thought she might die of embarrassment when all the kids started laughing.

But then one of the girls in the group said, "That color is so cool."

And another asked, "What's it got? A V8 engine?"

That's when Ashley realized that maybe they hadn't been laughing at her after all. "Yeah, I guess so," she replied as she started walking up to the school before anyone else asked her a truck question she couldn't answer. As Ashley followed the path, she noticed that there was a girl with long brown hair standing by the door, watching her. Once Ashley met her eyes, a warm smile spread across the girl's face.

"Ashley?" she called out. "Are you Ashley?"

"Yeah," Ashley replied.

"Welcome to Heaton Corners High!" the girl exclaimed. "I'm Mary Beth. Mary Beth Medina. My uncle sold your parents the farm. You met him—Chick Medina?"

"Right," Ashley said, nodding as she remembered the real estate agent who'd given her parents the keys to the farm yesterday, right before the moving truck had arrived.

"We're just so glad you guys moved to Heaton Corners!" Mary Beth said. "Now, I already got your schedule from the office, which is exactly the same as mine, so I can show you where all your classes are and stuff."

"Oh. Thanks," Ashley replied. "That's really nice of you. I have a superbad sense of direction. Like, the worst."

Mary Beth laughed. "Well, I'm pretty sure you won't get lost here," she said. "There's only forty kids in seventh grade, so there's just two classes for each period. If you're not in Mr. Thomas's English class, you're in Mrs. Franklin's."

"Wow," Ashley said. "Forty kids? I think there were, like, fifteen hundred kids in my last school."

"Seriously?" Mary Beth said. "There aren't even fifteen hundred people in Heaton Corners! Come on, we should get to homeroom before the bell rings."

Clang. Clang. Clang.

The tarnished brass bell in the tower rocked back and forth, issuing a low, haunting chime that was nothing like the electric bells at Ashley's old school.

"Or, like now!" Mary Beth laughed as she grabbed Ashley's wrist and pulled her toward the stairs. "Mr. Thomas is really strict about tardiness. He gives out demerits if you're not in your seat when the bell stops ringing. Let's hurry!"

Homeroom was on the second floor, where a tall,

bearded man stood next to the classroom that was closest to the stairs.

"Mornin', Mary Beth," he said; Ashley guessed that he was her new homeroom teacher. "And is this Miss McDowell?"

"Yes," Ashley replied.

"Yes, sir," he corrected her gently.

"Sorry. Yes, sir," she repeated, wondering when she'd stepped through a time warp.

"Welcome to Heaton Corners and Heaton Corners High!" he replied warmly. "We're glad to have you with us, Ashley. I'm Mr. Thomas, and I teach English and history here."

"And homeroom," joked Mary Beth.

"That's right," Mr. Thomas said with a smile. "Now, we've rearranged the seating a little so that you can sit next to Mary Beth. She's offered to show you around and make sure you have everything you need."

"Right over here," Mary Beth said. "My desk is by the window."

Ashley followed Mary Beth and sat in the empty desk next to her. She kept an eye on the door as the rest of the students filed into homeroom, joking and laughing just like the kids at her old school. Once the kids sat down, though, they stopped talking immediately, and moments later the brass bell stopped chiming. There weren't any loudspeakers on the walls, Ashley realized, as Mr. Thomas stepped in front of the class and cleared his throat.

"Good morning, class," Mr. Thomas announced. "As I'm sure you've all heard, we have a new student joining us today. I know you'll all do your best to make sure that Ashley feels welcome here in Heaton Corners."

Ashley tried not to blush as every person in the room turned to look at her. She stared down at her desk and ran her finger over the polished wood, which gleamed even though it had been nicked and scratched in various places. There were initials carved into the lower left corner: *L. S.*

When Mr. Thomas continued with the morning announcements, Ashley glanced up, sure that no one would be looking at her anymore.

She was wrong.

Two seats ahead and three rows over, there was a boy with short, sandy-colored hair and the most intense blue eyes Ashley had ever seen. Their eyes locked for one long moment, and Ashley's heart started to pound. Then he—whoever he was—looked straight ahead, focusing all his attention on Mr. Thomas.

Ashley tried to do the same, but it wasn't easy, not with her heart thudding so unevenly and the boy just within her line of vision. She could almost see his profile. She could definitely see the freckles scattered across the back of his neck.

He wasn't looking at you, she told herself. *He was looking out the window. Which is what everybody does during homeroom when they're totally bored.*

But no matter how much Ashley tried to convince herself that that was the case, she knew that it wasn't true.

The rest of the day was such a whirlwind of new teachers, classes, books, and kids that Ashley stumbled home in a bit of a daze—with a grin on her face that she couldn't get rid of. She felt like a celebrity at school—everyone treated her like she was the coolest girl they'd ever met. Mary Beth had been amazing all day, introducing Ashley to her two best friends, Danielle Ramos and

Stephanie Gloucester, and to the rest of the kids in their grade . . . even that cute guy from homeroom, whose name was Joey Carmichael and who happened to be Mary Beth's cousin. Ashley was pretty sure she'd played it cool in front of him, but now, walking home alone in the late-afternoon sunlight under the golden leaves that slowly drifted from the trees, she could let down her guard and smile as big as she wanted. It was official: Ashley had a big, huge, gigantic, *enormous* crush on Joey.

Ashley shook her head, as if to clear it, and paused as she reached Perseverance Creek. *Wait—is it right or left at the creek?* she wondered. *I . . . think . . . it's right? No. Left.* Ashley turned left, hoping that she was still heading in the correct direction. After a quarter mile, she breathed a sigh of relief when she reached the small sign that read RURAL ROUTE 13. The McDowells' farm was just over the next hill.

Ashley wasn't sure if it was her good mood or if the farm really did look beautiful from a distance, but she paused at the top of the hill and looked down on the cozy gray house, the cheerful red barn, the sloping fields that were overgrown with wildflowers. Her parents had big plans for plowing those fields and planting all kinds of vegetables and row after row of blueberry bushes. And they talked all the time about the livestock they wanted to own—sheep in the meadow, cows in the pasture, maybe even a pair of pigs. For a moment—just a moment—Ashley suddenly understood why they were so excited about living on a farm.

Then she set off down the hill, pausing at the mailbox that was nailed to the picket fence around the house. It had been a big deal, back in Atlanta, when her parents had finally given Ashley a key to the McDowells' mailbox in the lobby of their apartment building. This mailbox didn't even have a lock. Ashley peeked inside, but there wasn't any mail. Or else her parents had gotten it already.

Then she paused. Ashley knelt down to take a closer look at the wooden post beneath the mailbox. There was a strange symbol scrawled beneath it, like a sideways 8 with a thick lump in the middle. Ashley was almost positive that the symbol hadn't been there yesterday.

Weird, she thought. *Or did I just not notice it before?*

"Ashley!" Mrs. McDowell yelled, leaning out the kitchen window. "I was just about to go looking for you! I was afraid you got lost! Where have you been?"

"Sorry!" Ashley said as she slammed the mailbox shut. "I was hanging out with some people after school and I guess it got kind of late. What time is it, anyway?"

"Almost five!" Mrs. McDowell replied, an edge of annoyance to her voice now that Ashley was obviously not lost somewhere in the countryside.

"I said sorry."

"Can you come into the kitchen and help me, please?"

"Yeah. Be right there."

In the kitchen, Mrs. McDowell was surrounded by piles of cardboard boxes. "I'm trying to find a frying pan," she said with a sigh as she rummaged through a box.

"What's for dinner?" asked Ashley as she knelt down near a different box.

"Scrambled eggs, I guess," Mrs. McDowell said. "I went to the store this morning, but the kitchen's not really unpacked enough to manage anything else."

With her head bent over the box, Mrs. McDowell didn't notice the face Ashley made.

"Tell me all about your first day! How was it?" Mrs. McDowell continued.

"It was good! People here are so nice. Like, really, really nice. It's kind of surprising."

Mrs. McDowell laughed. "Sounds like we got you out of the city just in time if you're surprised by that."

"Har, har," Ashley said sarcastically. "Seriously, it's pretty old-fashioned here, isn't it?"

"I think so," Mrs. McDowell said, choosing her words carefully. "I like it. Did you meet some potential new friends?"

"Yeah. There's this one girl, Mary Beth, and she was supercool. I ate lunch with her and her friends. They seem—"

Just then the back door creaked open, and Ashley's dad walked into the house.

"Hey, Pumpkin, you're home! How was school?"

"Shoes," Mrs. McDowell said, pointing to his muddy boots. "Leave them at the back door, please."

"Whoops," Mr. McDowell said with a grin. He trudged back to the door and started removing his heavy work boots. Ashley noticed a smudge of grease on his forehead and thick crescents of mud under his fingernails. It was getting hard to remember that he used to wear a suit and tie to work every day.

"Did we *lose* a box of kitchen stuff?" Mrs. McDowell asked no one in particular. "This is ridiculous."

"Maybe we should have something else for dinner," Ashley said hopefully. "Something that doesn't need a frying pan. Hey! I know! What about the leftover pizza from last night?"

"That was my lunch," Mr. McDowell said ruefully.

Ding-dong!

All three McDowells turned to the front door.

"Now *who* could that be?" Mrs. McDowell said with a sigh of frustration.

"I'll go see," Ashley said as she used a box to pull herself up from the floor. When she opened the front door, she saw a middle-aged woman with coffee-colored hair standing on the porch. Mary Beth was standing next to her.

"You must be Ashley!" Mrs. Medina said. "Mary Beth has told me all about you! We thought that you and your parents might appreciate a nice home-cooked meal tonight. It's so hard to move in to a house."

"Hi. Thanks. Ma'am," Ashley stammered, trying to remember her best manners. She held the door open wide. "Please come in."

Mrs. Medina swept into the house as if she owned it, proudly holding a steaming casserole dish with two red-and-white checked potholders.

"Ashley? Who is— Oh, hello." Mrs. McDowell walked into the living room, followed by Mr. McDowell.

"Mom, this is Mary Beth, from school. And her mom," Ashley said quickly.

"Nice to meet you!" Mr. McDowell said in a hearty voice.

"I apologize for the mess in here," Mrs. McDowell said as she tried to smooth down her hair. "It's just a disaster."

"Not at all!" Mrs. Medina said with a bright smile. "We don't want to interrupt your evening. We just brought over a little supper for you. Chicken-tortilla casserole. My mother-in-law's recipe. It won first prize at the Harvest Days."

"Back in 1965!" Mary Beth whispered to Ashley. Then she handed her a brown paper bag. "I made these myself."

Ashley peeked into the bag and saw a stack of thick, chewy brownies wrapped in plastic wrap. "Awesome," she said.

"I'll just pop this into your oven so it's hot when you're ready to eat," said Mrs. Medina.

"Wait, I'll—" Mrs. McDowell said helplessly. But it was too late—Mrs. Medina had already wandered right into the messy kitchen.

"I'm so sorry. It really is awful in there—"

"Don't be silly," Mrs. Medina replied. "Tell you what. I'll come back tomorrow afternoon while Mary Beth has her flute lesson and help you get your kitchen to rights."

"That's so kind—but I'd hate for you to go to any trouble—"

"Nonsense! No trouble at all! That's what neighbors do! Now come along, Mary Beth, we've got to get back."

"Would you—like to stay for dinner?"

"Another time—I've got to get Bill's supper ready before he finishes his chores. We're all just so glad you've come to Heaton Corners! We haven't had a new family move here in what seems like forever. . . . Twenty years or more, it must be . . ." Mrs. Medina trailed off as she let herself out. "I'll be back tomorrow afternoon. Bye, now!"

"Bye!" Ashley and her parents called. Ashley grinned as Mary Beth waved from the walkway.

"Chicken-tortilla casserole!" Mrs. McDowell exclaimed. "I haven't had that since I was a little girl."

"Smells good," Mrs. McDowell said. "That was so nice of them. I see you what you mean, Pumpkin."

"Yeah," Ashley said, watching out the window as Mary Beth and her mom walked toward their car. As Mrs. Medina paused by the mailbox, Ashley squinted, trying to see her better in the fading twilight. Was Mrs. Medina looking at the symbol drawn on the mailbox post?

And was that a troubled scowl that crossed her face or just a trick of the light?

CHAPTER 3

The next afternoon, Ashley was leaving the schoolyard when she heard a voice call her name. She turned around to see Joey Carmichael standing behind her!

"Hey, Joey," Ashley said, hoping she sounded normal—and not like somebody who was falling head over heels for the cutest guy in Heaton Corners.

"You walking home?" Joey asked.

Ashley nodded. "Are you?"

"Nah," Joey replied. "My brother's going to pick me up, but he's late. As usual."

Ashley nodded again. *Get it together,* she told herself. *Think of something—anything!—to talk about.*

But that was easier said than done, especially when Joey was standing so close and looking right at her.

"So, anyway," Joey finally said, "I was wondering if anybody told you about Harvest Days yet?"

"Not really," Ashley said. "I mean, I heard somebody mention it, but I don't know anything about it."

"It's the best!" Joey exclaimed, and an enormous smile lit up his whole face. "It's this big festival that happens every October to, like, celebrate fall and the harvest and everything. This carnival rolls into town and brings all these great rides and games and stuff. It is seriously the best . . . and it's this weekend!"

"That sounds awesome," Ashley said, grinning back at him. "I *love* autumn, everything about it. Especially October. It's my favorite month because of—"

A blaring truck horn just a few feet away drowned out her voice.

Ashley turned to look—and missed how Joey had suddenly started to blush.

"Chuckles!" a teenage guy yelled from the truck. "Get over here! I'm not waiting another minute!"

As if to show that he meant it, the guy moved the truck forward a few feet.

"My brother," Joey mumbled.

"Did he just call you *Chuckles*?" Ashley asked.

"Forget it. So, uh, the Harvest Days? Maybe I'll see you there?" said Joey.

"Oh yeah. Absolutely," Ashley replied. "It sounds amazing!"

"Chuckles! Three—two—one—"

"All right! I'm coming!" Joey yelled. "See you tomorrow, Ashley."

"Bye, Joey," Ashley called after him. She stood there until the navy truck roared away.

Then she started walking home, wearing an even bigger smile on her face than the day before.

When Ashley got home from school, she was surprised to see an old man painting the fence around her house. He looked up as Ashley approached and raised a hand in greeting.

"Hello, young lady," he said. "I'm Mr. Wagner. I'll be helping your father over the next few weeks. Gotta get this old farm ready for winter."

"Nice to meet you, sir," Ashley said, staring at the mailbox. The post beneath it glistened with a sheen of white paint that was still wet; now there was no trace of the symbol that had been scrawled there. Ashley wished that she'd had a chance to show it to her parents, but it was too late now. She adjusted her backpack as she continued on to the house, where she found her mom and Mrs. Medina sipping tea on the front porch.

"Hi, Pumpkin!" Mrs. McDowell said with a smile. "How was school?"

"Great," Ashley replied. She couldn't wait to tell her mom all about the Harvest Days.

"Just wait until you see the kitchen," Mrs. McDowell gushed. "Mrs. Medina here is a miracle worker! She just zipped through like a tornado, getting everything in order. I don't know how she did it so fast."

"Nonsense," Mrs. Medina said modestly, but Ashley could see from the satisfied smile on her face that she agreed with every word Mrs. McDowell had said. Remembering the way Mrs. Medina had looked at the mailbox post yesterday, Ashley decided that there was no better time to ask her mother about the symbol she'd seen.

"Hey, Mom?" Ashley asked. "Did you see that thing on the post yesterday? Under the mailbox?"

Mrs. Medina's smile vanished as quickly as it had appeared.

Mrs. McDowell shook her head. "What was it? A bug?"

"No. It was some kind of symbol. Like a figure eight, but sideways."

"Hmm."

"Anyway, it's gone now. That guy—Mr. Wagner?—painted over it."

"Oh, you met Mr. Wagner? He stopped by this morning and offered to help us get the farm winterized. I don't think I ever saw your dad look so relieved before!"

"Winterized—what does that mean?"

"Well, repairing the barn door, for example, and fixing the shingles on the roof—you know, the loose ones. Painting anything that's due for a fresh coat of paint."

"Like the fence, I guess," Ashley said.

"Sure. Though I think I would've started with fixing the roof," Mrs. McDowell said.

"Well, Wally knows what he's doing," Mrs. Medina spoke up loudly. "Oh! I almost forgot to tell you! This weekend is the Heaton Corners Harvest Days Festival, and you all absolutely have to come."

"Sounds like fun," replied Mrs. McDowell.

"It's been a tradition here in Heaton Corners for as

long as anyone can remember," Mrs. Medina said. "You'll just love it. There's a quilting bee and a cake auction and a scarecrow-making contest for the children!"

"And rides?" Ashley spoke up. "I heard there were rides."

"So you know all about it already. Why am I not surprised?" Mrs. McDowell laughed. "Ash always has her ear to the ground."

"I don't know *all* about it," Ashley corrected her. "It's just this boy at school mentioned it."

"*Which* boy?" Mrs. Medina asked. Her voice sounded innocent, but the way her eyebrows arched told Ashley that she was very interested in the answer.

"Actually, Joey, your nephew," Ashley replied.

"Joey is a very *nice* young man," Mrs. Medina said, giving Mrs. McDowell a meaningful look. "His mother was my sister, but she died when Joey was just a little boy."

"I'm so sorry to hear—" Mrs. McDowell began, but Mrs. Medina just kept talking.

"It was unfortunate when John Carmichael remarried," she said. "He didn't choose wisely, and why he had to look for someone outside of Heaton Corners, I'll never understand. Every eligible woman in town would have loved to become the next Mrs. Carmichael."

Ashley turned to her mother. Mrs. McDowell raised her eyebrows, but Mrs. Medina didn't seem to notice. "I don't care what John says, Felicia Carmichael just doesn't fit in here. She never learned to just leave well enough alone."

"I don't believe I've had the pleasure of meeting her yet," Mrs. McDowell jumped in.

"You probably won't. John and his sons handle most of the farm's business. The Carmichaels have lived in Heaton Corners as long as any family. Their homestead is over on Jasper Road. They have the apple orchard? You'll want to go there for your apples, of course, especially pie apples. And speaking of baking, Julia, I'm hoping we can put you down for a cake?"

"Sorry?" Mrs. McDowell asked, jarred by the quick change of subject.

"Oh, for the cake auction at the festival, of course," Mrs. Medina said. "All the money we raise goes to the Heaton High Scholarship Foundation. It's for *such* a good cause, and seeing as your kitchen is all set up—"

"I wish I could help, but I'm not much of a—"

"Thank you, Julia!" Mrs. Medina said. "Just bring

your cake to the high school by ten a.m. this Saturday. Oh, and a word to the wise—we've found that the triple-layer cakes tend to be the most impressive ones."

"Triple layer. Gotcha," Ashley's mom said with a thin smile.

"I'd better head off," Mrs. Medina said smoothly. "Mary Beth's flute lesson will be over in a few minutes."

"Thanks again for all your help," Mrs. McDowell said.

"Bye, Mrs. Medina," Ashley chimed in. "Say hi to Mary Beth for me."

"Of course, dear!"

Ashley and her mom watched as Mrs. Medina walked down the path. She stopped for a moment near Mr. Wagner and said something to him. Then he looked back at the house, tipped his hat at Ashley and Mrs. McDowell, and got into Mrs. Medina's car.

As they drove away, Ashley turned to her mother and raised her eyebrows. There was so much she wanted to say about Mrs. Medina's visit, but the first thing was, "A *cake*? A *triple-layer* cake? Mom, what were you thinking? You can't even make a birthday cake!"

"Yes, I can!" Mrs. McDowell protested.

Ashley started to laugh. "Mom. A pile of doughnuts

with a candle stuck in them is *not* a birthday cake."

"Oh, *excuse* me," Mrs. McDowell said, but Ashley could tell from her smile that she was kidding. Ashley giggled.

"Ash, what am I going to do?" her mom said with a groan. "I'm not even sure we own a cake pan!"

"Don't worry, I have it all figured out," Ashley replied. "We'll just buy a cake. Like, a really nice one from a bakery or something."

"Yeah, right. That would be a scandal that Heaton Corners would be buzzing about for *years*," Mrs. McDowell replied. "I don't get the impression they really go for store-bought baked goods around here."

"Okay . . ." Ashley said. "Well, what if we bought the cake but decorated it ourselves? We could make it look really amazing . . . like, with a spooky theme or something."

"That's not a bad idea," Mrs. McDowell said. "Actually, it's a great idea. I think we could handle that!"

"Is the cable hooked up yet?" Ashley asked hopefully. "We could look up some pictures on the Internet."

"Not yet, honey," Mrs. McDowell said. "We've been having a little trouble with that. It seems that Heaton

Corners isn't exactly an Internet hot spot. But your dad's on the case, and hopefully the Internet should be set up tomorrow. So anyway—tell me about Joey."

"Not much to tell," Ashley said with a shrug. "He's just a boy. He told me about the Harvest Days Festival and asked if I was going."

"I was sorry to hear about his mother," said Mrs. McDowell. "It's hard losing a parent so young. I hope his stepmother is a nice person."

"Me too," said Ashley. "I wonder what Mrs. Medina's problem with her is."

"Who knows?" replied Mrs. McDowell. "Sometimes people in small towns can be too into each others' business. It's best to just ignore gossip. So . . . did he ask you to go with him . . . to the festival?"

"Oh no," Ashley said right away. "It was nothing like that. He was just telling me about it. Since everyone goes, I guess."

"Are you sure?" Mrs. McDowell asked.

"Definitely."

Mrs. McDowell looked at Ashley for a long moment. "Okay."

"So, anyway," Ashley said, eager to change the

subject. "I guess I'll start my homework."

"Okay," Mrs. McDowell repeated.

As Ashley slung her backpack over her shoulder, she couldn't help wondering if her mom was on to something. *Maybe Joey* was *going to ask me to go with him,* she thought. *Maybe he would've if his brother hadn't driven up at that moment!*

Then Ashley smiled to herself. There was no harm in wishing that Joey liked her too.

After all, sometimes wishes came true.

On Saturday morning—the day of the festival—the lights were on at the McDowells' house before the sun was up. Ashley and her mom had spent the last three hours hunched over the chocolate sheet cake Mrs. McDowell had bought the day before.

"It looks good, Mom," Ashley said, stifling a yawn.

Mrs. McDowell frowned and adjusted a gummy worm. "You think so?" she asked anxiously. "I wish I'd bought more of those little sugar pumpkins. Too late now—I don't have time to drive all the way to the big supermarket in Walthrop to get more."

"No, it really looks amazing," Ashley assured her mother. They had decorated the cake to look like a spooky cemetery, with crooked cookie tombstones and grass made from shredded coconut that they had dyed with green food coloring. Ashley's favorite part was adding the Halloween candy her mom had bought. Marshmallow ghosts peeked around the cookie tombstones, and licorice bats flew above them, suspended by nearly invisible fishing wire that hung down from a cardboard overhang that Ashley had painted to look like a haunted forest.

"I mean, who wouldn't love this cake?" Ashley asked.

"I love this cake!" Mr. McDowell said as he poured himself another cup of coffee. "Really, ladies, you outdid yourselves."

Mrs. McDowell stood back to admire their efforts. "It does look pretty good, doesn't it?"

"The best," Ashley said firmly.

"Yikes—quarter of ten! We've got to leave so we can drop off the cake on time," Mrs. McDowell exclaimed as she glanced at the clock. "Everybody ready to go?"

"Hang on," Ashley said. "I have to change."

She rushed up the stairs to her bedroom and pulled

on her favorite sweater, an orange one that was just a few shades lighter than her auburn hair. Then Ashley dashed into the bathroom to brush her hair and apply a touch of apple-flavored lip gloss. She stared at her reflection in the mirror and smiled wide to make sure she didn't have any lip gloss on her teeth.

When the McDowells arrived at the high school a few minutes later, Ashley couldn't believe how many people were there. "Look at this!" she exclaimed. "I didn't know this many people even *lived* in Heaton Corners!"

"Neither did I," said Mr. McDowell. "Parking is going to be impossible. Ash, how about you get out here so you can bring in the cake? We'll meet you at the flagpole after I find a parking spot."

"Okay, Dad," Ashley said. "See you in a few minutes."

As she walked up the steps of the high school, Ashley noticed that everyone she passed by stopped and stared at the cake. *I knew it!* she thought. *Our cake really did turn out amazing!* She couldn't wait to find out how much it would bring in for the scholarship fund.

Inside the cafeteria, Ashley carried the cake over to a long table that was crowded with towering cakes—vanilla, chocolate, coconut, jelly roll, apple, and even a pineapple upside-down cake. But none of the other cakes, Ashley noticed proudly, had such festive and original decorations.

The two women standing behind the table froze when Ashley approached them.

"What is *that*?" one of them asked.

"It's for the auction," Ashley replied. "Mrs. Medina asked my mom to make it?"

"Of course," the other woman said quickly as she reached for the cake. "Thank you, dear. You run along and enjoy the fair."

Ashley turned away to leave, but she couldn't help overhearing what the women said next.

"Cynthia, we shouldn't—"

"They're the *new* family. Obviously they don't *know*—"

But when Ashley turned around again to see what the problem was, the women smiled brightly at her—as if nothing was wrong.

Well, so what if we didn't make some lame old-fashioned three-layer cake? Ashley thought defensively as she walked outside into the bright October sunshine. Even more people had arrived on the school grounds while she was inside. By the time Ashley made it through the crowd to the flagpole, her parents were waiting for her.

"Everything go okay?" Mrs. McDowell asked. "With dropping off the cake?"

"Oh, definitely," Ashley said. She knew that she could never tell her mother about the way those two women had behaved. Her mom was so proud of that cake. She'd be completely humiliated if she knew that those women had acted as if Ashley'd brought them a platter of trash.

"Ashley! Hey!" Mary Beth called over as she ran up to the flagpole. Stephanie and Danielle were right behind her.

"Hey, you guys!" Ashley said before she introduced her parents to the other girls. Then she turned to her mom. "Is it okay if I hang out with them?"

"Of course," Mrs. McDowell said. "The cake auction is at three o'clock. I'll see you there, right?"

"Wouldn't miss it!" Ashley replied. "Bye!"

Then the girls hurried around to the football field, where all the rides and games were set up. They built a hilarious scarecrow with a Mohawk made out of hay, and then they rode the Tilt-A-Whirl four times in a row. But no matter what they did, Ashley kept an eye out for

Joey in the crowd, even when she and her friends were riding the Ferris wheel that towered over the rest of the fair. Just as she was starting to think that maybe Joey had skipped the festival . . .

There he was.

Standing right in front of the Ferris wheel!

Joey noticed her at the same time and raised a hand in greeting. By the time the ride ended and Ashley climbed out of the metal bucket, she was sure of it: Joey was waiting for her.

"Hey," Joey said.

"Hey, Joey," Ashley replied. "I thought maybe you weren't going to make it."

The minute the words were out of her mouth, Ashley wished she could take them back. But Joey didn't seem to realize that she'd just admitted she'd been looking—waiting—for him.

"Oh yeah. I was stuck at the apple judging," Joey said, shaking his head. "Every year my dad wins first prize, and every year he makes Pete and me stand around with him and the apples until the judges award the ribbons. I guess it really drives home the 'family farm' thing."

"Congratulations, huh? First prize apples, that's

pretty cool. I'll have to try one," Ashley said.

"Oh, definitely," Joey replied, giving Ashley that slow, warm smile that made her feel all fluttery and nervous inside. At that same moment, Mary Beth, Stephanie, and Danielle walked up. "So, where are you all headed now?" Joey asked the group.

"Actually, I was wondering where the haunted house is," Ashley said, turning to her friends. "I hope it's really scary!"

"Haunted what?" asked Stephanie.

"You know," Ashley said. "The haunted house."

But the others kids just stared at her blankly.

"Why would there be one of those at the harvest festival?" Danielle asked.

"Well, because it's October," Ashley said. "You know, Halloween and all that. I'm kind of surprised that there aren't more jack-o'-lanterns and stuff at the festival. Maybe all the farmers are saving the pumpkins for Halloween night?"

"We don't really do Halloween in Heaton Corners," Mary Beth explained.

Ashley couldn't help it; her jaw dropped open. She felt like she was talking to visitors from another planet.

"You don't do Halloween? It's my favorite holiday!"

Mary Beth shrugged. "I know it's a big deal in other towns, but not here. I guess October in Heaton Corners is more about the harvest than frights and stuff like that."

"Oh, man," Ashley said, totally bummed out. "Halloween is the best. I love getting dressed up—I always go for the superscariest costume I can think of. And trick-or-treating is so much fun. The candy, the chill in the air, the decorations . . . " She shivered with excitement as she got lost in her thoughts. "It's absolutely my favorite night of the year."

"I guess I've never really given Halloween much thought before," said Danielle, "but that sounds like a lot of fun. I wish we could go trick-or-treating."

"This year we *so* will," Ashley said. "Because I'm not going to miss trick-or-treating for anything. We'll all go together!"

"No, you won't."

At the sound of Joey's voice, Ashley turned to look at him. His handsome face was contorted by such a scowl that it was like a dark cloud had passed over the sun, obliterating all its warmth and light.

"Huh?" Ashley asked, sure that she had misheard him.

"No, you won't," Joey repeated. "You won't go trick-or-treating. Nobody goes trick-or-treating in Heaton Corners, and nobody ever will."

Mary Beth scowled at her cousin. "I don't exactly know what your problem is, Joey," she said calmly, "but we'll do whatever we want. And nobody—especially not *you*—can stop us."

Then she locked arms with Ashley and spun around. The two girls started to walk away. Danielle and Stephanie followed, leaving Joey standing alone in the middle of the Harvest Days Festival.

If Ashley had turned around to look at him, she would've seen that there was something more than anger in his face: complete and total fear.

CHAPTER 4

"What was that?" Ashley asked, once the girls were a safe distance away from Joey.

"Ugh, I don't know," Mary Beth replied, shaking her head.

"He just got so intense," Ashley remarked.

Mary Beth continued to shake her head. "He can be so weird sometimes. Ever since his father remarried."

Ashley didn't know what to say. "Bummer. He seemed so nice."

Mary Beth gave her such a sharp look that it made Ashley's cheeks turn pink. "Do you *like* him?" she asked.

"I don't know," Ashley said, breaking out into a grin despite herself. "Maybe. Just a little. It's no big deal."

Just then Danielle and Stephanie caught up to them,

and Ashley sent Mary Beth a desperate signal with her eyes that said *please don't say anything*.

And from Mary Beth's smile, kind and reassuring, Ashley knew that she wouldn't.

"Hey," Mary Beth said. "It's almost time for the cake auction! Let's go check it out!"

She led the other girls into the auditorium, which was almost full. "I can't believe all these people showed up just to bid on cakes," Ashley said with a giggle.

"You'd be surprised," Stephanie replied. "The people in Heaton Corners really love cake."

"Like, *really* love cake," Danielle added. "The auction can get a little wild."

"Wild?" Ashley repeated. "A wild *cake auction*?"

"Don't say we didn't warn you!" Mary Beth told her.

Just then Ashley spotted her mom in the audience, waving at her. Ashley grimaced before giving her mom a little wave, hoping that her mom would get the hint and stop making such a scene. Luckily for Ashley, Mrs. Medina took the stage, and the cake auction began. Ashley soon realized that her friends had been right: People were jumping out of their seats, shouting their bids, and flailing their arms in the air. Ashley waited expectantly as, one by one, the cakes she'd seen that morning were auctioned off to the highest bidder. After each one, she figured that surely the haunted-cemetery cake she and her mom had decorated would come next.

Then Mrs. Medina said something that made Ashley's heart start to race.

"Ladies and gentlemen," she began, "you know I hate to play favorites, but this year we have truly saved the best cake for last."

Oh, wow! Ashley thought, the butterflies churning in her stomach. *She's talking about* our *cake!* Our *cake!*

Across the auditorium, Mrs. McDowell caught Ashley's eye. She had the biggest smile on her face—the kind that made her nose go all crinkly.

"So without further ado, allow me to present," Mrs. Medina continued, pausing for dramatic effect, "Margaret Pierce's coconut cake with pineapple filling! This tropical treat will send your taste buds on vacation. The whipped cream frosting is . . ."

Mrs. Medina kept describing the cake, but Ashley had already tuned her out. She was trying to understand *what*, exactly, had just happened. The last cake was being auctioned off . . . but where was the cake Ashley had decorated with her mom?

As the sound of applause thundered in her ears, Ashley realized that the auction was over. She glanced at her mom. Mrs. McDowell kept a big smile on her face, but Ashley could tell from the tightness around her eyes that she was disappointed . . . and embarrassed. A flash of indignation burned in Ashley's chest. *It's not right,* she thought. *We went to a lot of trouble to make that cake.*

"I'll be right back," Ashley said to Mary Beth.

Then she marched over to Mrs. Medina.

"Mrs. Medina?" she said. "Um, excuse me, Mrs. Medina . . . ma'am?"

"Yes, Ashley?" Mrs. Medina asked.

"I, um, I didn't see my mom's cake in the auction," Ashley said. "What happened?"

"Oh, that? There was a cake accident," Mrs. Medina said. "I'm afraid we couldn't auction off the cake you . . . decorated. But we surely do appreciate your efforts."

"A cake accident?" Ashley repeated.

"Yes. You know. These things happen," Mrs. Medina replied, waving her hand in the air like it didn't matter at all. Then she turned away to talk to someone else.

Ashley realized that Mrs. Medina had nothing more

to say on the subject. But she couldn't shake the feeling there was something important that Mrs. Medina was leaving out. And it made Ashley begin to suspect there was something not quite right about Heaton Corners—and the people who called it home.

"They must have tasted it," Ashley's mom blurted out in the car later that afternoon. "They must have figured out that we bought the cake."

Ashley shook her head. "I don't know, Mom. From what Mrs. Medina said, I got the feeling there was something she wasn't telling me. I'm starting to think Heaton Corners is kinda weird."

Ashley's mom moaned. "No, the only thing that's weird is that the people here are very polite—too polite to say anything rude about my shortcut. After all, look how hard they worked on their cakes!"

Ashley's dad smiled reassuringly. "Don't beat yourself up about it. I'm sure everyone will forget about it, and by next year your cake will be the star of their silly auction."

Mrs. McDowell sighed. "I'm so embarrassed. Just don't say anything to Mary Beth about it, okay, Ash?"

Ashley nodded, but she wasn't convinced by what her mom had said. Mrs. Medina seemed like a woman who always said what was on her mind. There had to be something she was keeping secret . . . something Ashley was determined to find out.

But as October hurried on, the cake incident slipped from Ashley's mind. Between homework, tests, unpacking her room, and hanging out with her new friends, it wasn't long before the end of the month came around.

"You know what happens in five days?" Ashley asked her friends at lunch one afternoon.

"Halloween!" replied Mary Beth. "I've been counting down the days, ever since the Harvest Days Festival!"

"I know!" Ashley replied. "I can't believe it's so soon. I still haven't figured out what to wear for my costume!"

Danielle and Stephanie exchanged a glance that was impossible for Ashley to miss.

"We're on for trick-or-treating, right?" Ashley asked.

Danielle looked down. "It definitely sounds like fun, but nobody really celebrates Halloween here, so what's the point of going trick-or-treating?"

"Almost nobody," Mary Beth added, and the other girls turned to look at her. She shrugged. "What? Haven't you ever looked out your window on Halloween night? I've seen . . . what do you call them, Ashley? Tricky treaters?"

"Trick-*or*-treaters," Ashley corrected her.

Mary Beth continued, "Well, whatever you call them, I've seen them out my window. It looks like fun—it's too bad my mom never lets me leave the house to join them. Well, this year will be different. Count me in, Ash."

Ashley turned to Stephanie and Danielle. "Come on! We'll have the best time . . . and who knows, maybe people will start celebrating Halloween in Heaton Corners after we show them how much fun it is."

Ashley grinned as Danielle and Stephanie began to nod. Mary Beth clapped her hands together in delight. "Awesome! I can't wait. Now we just need to figure out a way to convince our parents to let us go trick-or-treating!"

Since Ashley's parents were spending the afternoon at a tractor show in Walthrop, she decided to start her homework in the library after school. She would never admit it, but she wasn't quite comfortable staying alone in the creaky old farmhouse yet. By the time Ashley finished her science homework, the sun was starting to set, and she knew she'd better hurry before it was too dark to see the path home.

As she packed up her books, Ashley's stomach started to growl. She searched her backpack for a granola bar to snack on while she walked, but all she found was a piece of cinnamon-flavored gum.

Then Ashley remembered the small corner store that was a block and a half from school. It was out of her way, but if she hurried, she could buy a candy bar for the walk home. *Maybe they'll have those awesome chocolate-dipped marshmallow pumpkins,* Ashley thought hopefully. It was just her luck that her favorite kind of candy in the whole world was only available for a couple of weeks a year.

A dry, dusty wind swirled around Ashley as she started down the steps of the school; instinctively, she wrapped her arms around herself and shivered inside her green corduroy jacket. In a few minutes she reached the corner store. A hand-painted sign in the window read:

HEATON CORNERS
GROCERY AND DRY GOODS

A tiny cluster of bells tinkled as Ashley opened the door. It was a small store, with four narrow aisles and an ancient-looking refrigerator case along the back wall. Ashley prowled the aisles looking for a display of Halloween candy, but within moments she realized that the store didn't have one. In fact, it didn't seem to have any Halloween candy at all.

"Help you?" someone with a scratchy voice called out.

Ashley jumped; she hadn't seen anyone when she'd walked in, but now she realized that an old woman—easily the oldest woman she'd seen in Heaton Corners—was sitting behind the scratched glass counter at the front of the store. Her hair was the color of wet ashes and so snarled and unkempt that it looked like she hadn't brushed it in weeks—maybe months. The woman sat hunched over on a tall wooden stool, stroking a cat with fur so black that it blended right into the loose tunic the woman wore.

"Oh!" Ashley cried in surprise. Then she smiled. "Your cat is so beautiful! May I pet it? Is it friendly?"

"Which one?" the woman asked, and let out an almost growling sound from the very back of her throat. To Ashley's delight, three more cats—each one black as ink—suddenly appeared from different corners of the store. They hopped up onto the counter, purring loudly as the woman scratched their chins and rubbed behind their ears.

"Oh, they're so sweet," Ashley said longingly. She'd always wanted a cat. *I have to remember to ask Mom and Dad about that,* she thought. *Aren't cats supposed to be really useful on farms?*

"What's your name, dearie? I haven't seen you in here before," the woman said.

"I'm Ashley. We just moved here a few weeks ago."

"You can call me Miss Bernice."

"It's nice to meet you, ma'am," Ashley said, marveling at how much she sounded like Mary Beth just then.

Miss Bernice nodded, pleased. "My cats know you're a good person," she said, shaking a gnarled finger in Ashley's direction. "I never meet a person until my cats size them up first, you know. I won't waste my time on someone if my cats won't waste theirs."

Ashley smiled as one of the cats nuzzled against her shoulder. The lady was pretty eccentric, but she seemed harmless enough.

"Was there something in particular you were looking for?" Miss Bernice asked.

"Yeah, kind of," Ashley replied. "Do you have chocolate-dipped marshmallow pumpkins? The kind they make for Halloween?"

Miss Bernice's mouth transformed from a smile to a snarl, and her lips curled back to reveal teeth so yellowed and wide set, they looked like whittled chunks of wood. "You think I'd sell Halloween candy here?" she asked in a dangerously quiet voice.

"I'm sorry?" Ashley asked in confusion.

"I would never do that!" Miss Bernice cried. "I never would! Never, never, never!"

Each time she said the word "never," the volume and pitch of Miss Bernice's voice rose. Then she slammed her hands on the counter so hard that Ashley jumped. So did the cats—and one of them knocked over a display of glass soda bottles. A dozen bottles crashed to the floor and shattered, spilling a pool of dark, carbonated liquid over the dingy tiles.

"Oh, Clatter!" Miss Bernice shrieked at the cat. "Look at what you've done!" She shuffled around the counter and slowly lowered herself to the floor, as if it hurt to bend her knees.

Even though Ashley was totally freaked out by

Miss Bernice's outburst, she knew she couldn't leave the elderly lady to clean up the mess all by herself. "Here, I can help," she said awkwardly. "Do you have a sponge or a, uh, mop or something?"

"Back corner," Miss Bernice replied. "There are cleaning supplies in the bathroom."

Ashley scurried off to the far corner of the store, where she found a door that led to a bathroom. A variety of brooms and mops were stacked against one wall of the clean yet cramped room. As Ashley sorted through the mops, she realized that they weren't leaning on the wall.

They were propped against a narrow wooden door.

As her hand brushed against the cold brass doorknob, Ashley took a closer look. There, scratched into the wood of the door, was a sideways figure eight.

It looked exactly like the symbol that someone had drawn on the McDowells' fence right after they had moved in.

Ashley sneaked a fast glance over her shoulder, but she was confident that Miss Bernice hadn't followed her back here—not after the way she'd moved so slowly and gingerly when the spill had happened.

You shouldn't open that door, Ashley told herself,

remembering all the times her mother had told her not to poke around behind closed doors. *Don't be nosy.*

And yet, it seemed impossible to walk away.

Maybe it's a broom closet, Ashley suddenly thought. *Maybe there's spray cleaner and sponges and stuff in there.*

But she had a funny feeling, deep inside, that that wouldn't be the case.

She rested her hand on the doorknob, took a breath, and slowly turned it. Then she eased the door open, waiting for the telltale creak of rusty hinges that would announce to Miss Bernice that she was snooping around.

The door, however, swung open easily, silently, as if it was often used. Without wasting another moment, Ashley slipped inside and snapped on the light.

It was a small room, without any furniture or windows. The walls were covered with faded, yellowing wallpaper and dozens of names written on slips of paper, each one tacked to the wall in a random pattern.

Are these nothing more than the delusions of a crazy woman, Ashley asked herself, *or is this "list" something more?*

Then she felt a faint breath of air on her neck, as if someone, hovering just behind her, had sighed, softly and sadly.

Ashley spun around, sure that Miss Bernice had followed her after all, bracing for the scolding.

But no one was there.

Ashley didn't waste another moment in that tiny, secret room. She shut the door, wishing that she could shut away her memory of those scrawled names as easily. Then she grabbed a mop and hurried back to the front of the store.

As the strands of the mop soaked up the spilled soda, Ashley couldn't help worrying that somehow Miss Bernice would know she had seen what was hidden behind the marked door. But if Miss Bernice had any idea that Ashley had been poking around back there, she didn't mention it.

"Sorry about the spill," Ashley mumbled when she was finished with the mop—even though it hadn't been her fault. When she put the mop away, she didn't even glance at the door behind the cleaning supplies.

Just as Ashley was about to leave, Miss Bernice thrust out a wrinkled hand and grabbed Ashley's wrist. She held on so tightly that Ashley could feel Miss Bernice's stiffened finger bones right though the thick corduroy of her coat.

"You don't go trick-or-treating in this town, Ashley McDowell," Miss Bernice told her. It was not a command, or a suggestion, but a warning. "It's dangerous to do so. Nobody trick-or-treats in Heaton Corners. You'd be wise to heed what I'm telling you. Are you listening to me? Do you hear what I'm saying to you? You don't go trick-or-treating in Heaton Corners!"

Ashley yanked her arm away from Miss Bernice's grasp and ran out into the twilight.

She was halfway home before she remembered that she hadn't told Miss Bernice her last name.

CHAPTER 5

Bliiip!

Ashley grinned at the monitor as she accepted the incoming video chat. "Maya-oh-Maya!" she trilled.

"Hey, sis!" Ashley's big sister, Maya, said, grinning back at her.

After a few weeks of spotty Internet, Ashley's computer was finally connecting quickly enough for her to chat with Maya. It was the longest they'd ever gone without seeing each other. As soon as Ashley saw Maya's face, she felt at home—for the first time—in Heaton Corners.

"How are you? I've been missing you like crazy!" Ashley said.

"Me? Oh, I'm just drowning in homework, no big,"

Maya replied, widening her eyes. "Seriously, I was up until four a.m. last night reading."

"Are you kidding me?" Ashley gasped.

"Well, it probably wouldn't have been quite so late, but my roommate and I started watching movies at midnight," Maya admitted. "So. You know."

"College sounds *awesome*," Ashley said.

"It is. A lot of work, though," Maya said. "But enough about my boring life. How's the new house? The new town? Tell me *everything*."

"It's not bad," Ashley told her sister. "I mean, it's still kind of weird. Do you know where Mom and Dad went yesterday? A *tractor show*. No lie."

Maya started to crack up. "So they're really doing this whole farmer thing, huh? Old McDowell had a farm, e-i-e-i-o!"

"They seem really happy here," Ashley said.

"And what about you?" Maya asked. "Are you happy in Heaton Corners?"

"I'm getting used to it," Ashley replied. "The people here are incredibly nice. I already made a ton of friends at school."

"Go you!" Maya said. "Miss Popularity, huh?"

"Well, I wouldn't go that far," Ashley replied. Then she paused, trying to figure out if she should tell Maya about some of the stranger things about Heaton Corners. Of course, Maya knew her well enough that the moment Ashley hesitated, she could tell that something was going on.

"What?" Maya asked in a voice that told Ashley she could spill it all.

"Here's something crazy," Ashley finally said. "They, like, don't have Halloween here."

"Huh?" Maya asked. "What does that mean?"

"It means that nobody celebrates Halloween," Ashley tried to explain.

Maya looked like she was having a hard time believing her. "For real? That is just bizarre."

"Right?" said Ashley. "I went to this store, and they don't even sell Halloween candy. This old lady practically freaked out at me when I asked for some." Ashley didn't mention the secret room or all the spooky names plastered on its yellowed walls.

"What? No chocolate-dipped marshmallow pumpkins for Mom and Dad's Pumpkin?" Maya exclaimed. "That should be against the law!"

"Totally."

"You're still going to get dressed up, right?" Maya said.

"Absolutely," Ashley replied right away. "Heaton Corners has its traditions and I have mine . . . and that includes Halloween. But I need to get started on my costume tonight, because, you know, they definitely don't sell Halloween costumes here. I think I *finally* figured out how to attach the—"

"Stop, stop, stop!" Maya begged, clapping her hands over her ears. "I got your text about it, and, seriously, that is all I need to know. No details, no pictures, no nothing. It's way too creepy."

"Hello? It's Halloween. That's the whole point!" But Ashley had to smile. If she had freaked out Maya with a simple text about her costume idea, then Ashley knew she was on the right track.

"And something else special is coming up, I know," Maya said, quickly changing the subject. "Ash, I'm so sorry. I really wanted to come home for your birthday, but I have a midterm the next day. I've got to stay here and study my head off."

"That's cool. I understand," Ashley said—but

she couldn't help thinking how absolutely amazing it would've been if Maya could have come home to help celebrate her birthday.

"I'm going to send you an extra-special present," Maya promised her.

"Ooh, what? What?"

"Uh-uh," Maya said, shaking her head. "It's a surprise. You'll just have to wait."

"Oh fine." Ashley sighed. "You're still coming home for Thanksgiving, right?"

"If they celebrate it in Heaton Corners!" Maya joked. "But seriously, I will so be there. I can't wait to see the new house and the farm and everything. Will we have to harvest our own cranberries from some bog or something?"

"Hey, be careful you don't give Mom any ideas!" Ashley giggled.

Maya looked at her watch. "I should probably get going soon, little sis."

"One more thing, Maya? There's one other kind of weird thing I've noticed around here."

"What's that?"

"It's this mysterious symbol," Ashley said. "It looks

like a sideways eight. Here, I'll show you."

Ashley quickly scrawled the symbol on a page of her notebook and held it up to the camera for Maya to see.

"Oh, that?" Maya said right away. "That's not mysterious. It's a lemniscate."

"A lemnon-what?"

"A *lemniscate*," Maya repeated. "The symbol for infinity. It's all over my calculus textbook."

"Oh," Ashley said, feeling a little silly for thinking there was something special about the symbol.

"I mean, it's almost a lemniscate," Maya continued as she peered at the screen. "A real lemniscate doesn't have that thick lump in the middle of it. Where'd you see it?"

"Just a couple places." Ashley shrugged. "Like, there was one on our mailbox post before it got painted over."

"Graffiti, Heaton Corners–style." Maya laughed. "Sounds pretty tame, honestly."

"Yeah, maybe by Chicago standards," Ashley said. "But it's weird for here. I mean, everybody has a perfect little white fence, these cute little flower boxes, American flags fluttering in the breeze. It's kind of hard to believe that *anybody* here would be into graffiti."

"You'd be surprised," Maya said. "Small towns aren't

that different from big cities. People are people, you know?"

"I guess."

"Listen, Ash, I really gotta go. I'm meeting some people at the library for study group," Maya said. "Let's chat again soon, okay?"

"Any time," Ashley said. "Seriously, any time you want. I miss you so much. So, so, so, so, sooooooooooooo much."

"I miss you too," Maya said, blowing a bunch of kisses at her computer. "Text me whenever, okay?"

"I will. Talk to you soon," Ashley replied, blowing some kisses back at Maya.

Bliiip!

Maya's window went black an instant before it disappeared, and Ashley missed her sister more than ever as she stared at the blank screen. She picked up her pen and started doodling on a page of her notebook, scrawling the same image over and over as her mind wandered.

Only later did Ashley realize that she'd filled the page with dozens of lemniscates.

The next day, Wednesday, Ashley stopped by her locker to grab her lunch before she met Mary Beth and the rest of the girls in the cafeteria. But her locker was not the way she had left it.

There was a brown paper bag taped to it. The bag bulged slightly at the bottom, as if it had something heavy inside it, and whoever had taped it to Ashley's locker had used a *lot* of tape, as if they'd wanted to make sure the bag wouldn't fall off. It took her forever to remove all the tape, her anticipation growing so strong that her hands shook a little bit when she finally pulled down the bag.

The bag crinkled as she unfolded the flap and peeked inside. Ashley didn't know what, exactly, she expected to see, but she couldn't have been more surprised to find a single apple at the bottom of the bag. There was no note, no name, just a perfectly round, perfectly red apple. Ashley pulled the apple out of the bag and held it close to her face, feeling the glossy skin and smelling its faint, sweet scent. It really was a beautiful apple—heavy and fresh, without a single flaw or blemish.

Who left me this apple? she wondered.

But already Ashley had her suspicions. After all, who

in Heaton Corners lived on an actual apple orchard? A wide smile stretched across her face as she imagined Joey picking out the best apple he could find before school. Joey, sneaking over to her locker while everyone else was in class. Joey, using half a role of tape to make sure that the apple wouldn't fall to the floor before Ashley could find it.

They hadn't really talked since the weirdness at the Harvest Days Festival, but sometimes Ashley still felt like Joey was looking at her.

At least, she wished that he was still looking at her.

Maybe this is a sign, she thought. *Maybe this is a sign from him that he's sorry. Maybe we can just forget that whole thing.*

Ashley was still grinning when she got to the cafeteria. She was feeling great about Heaton Corners. So what if the people here were a little weird about Halloween? She had a crush on the cutest boy ever, and she suspected he had a crush on her too. And she had an awesome group of friends who were waving to her excitedly from their usual table.

"Ash! What took you so long?" Danielle asked, scooting over to make room for Ashley on the long wooden bench.

"No reason," Ashley said with a shrug, and winked

at Mary Beth. Mary Beth might not always get along with her cousin, but Ashley couldn't wait to gush about Joey with her later. Maybe her mom would let Mary Beth sleep over this weekend.

And then, in a flash of inspiration, Ashley had a brilliant idea. It was so obvious. Why hadn't she thought of it before?

"So I was wondering," Ashley began. "About Halloween? See, it's not just my favorite holiday—it's also my birthday."

"Why didn't you say anything before?" asked Danielle.

"Oh, well, I don't know," Ashley began. "I'm new and I didn't want you guys to feel like you have to celebrate with me—"

"But we'd love to," Stephanie interrupted.

"Well in that case," said Ashley, and then she just launched into it, "do you guys want to come over to my house for a birthday sleepover party? On Halloween? We can go trick-or-treating, and no one will even have to know."

Mary Beth spoke first. "That. Is. Brilliant." Danielle and Stephanie nodded excitedly.

"Yay!" Ashley squealed.

"I won't have to beg my mom to let me go trick-or-treating," Mary Beth continued. "I'll just tell her I'm coming to your birthday party."

"It's not even a lie," Ashley said.

"No, definitely not," said Mary Beth. "But if my mom finds out, she will ground me so hard, you'll probably never see me again."

"Well, if this is your last party ever, we'd better make it count." Danielle giggled.

"And speaking of making it count . . . we need to talk costumes!" Ashley announced. "I have one rule, okay? Anything goes—but it has to be *scary*. None of this fancy movie star or frilly princess stuff."

Mary Beth pulled her notebook out of her backpack and started sketching. "So . . . scary costumes," she began. "Like, a witch would be okay, right?"

"You could make it really scary," Stephanie said. "Like, horrible claw hands with long nails and a face full of warts!"

Mary Beth wrinkled her nose. "I don't know if I want a face full of warts," she replied.

"What about a vampire?" Danielle suggested. "But you would need some blood."

"There are tons of easy fake-blood recipes on the Internet," Ashley advised.

"That's great, but our families aren't hooked up to the Internet, remember?" Danielle replied.

Ashley couldn't believe she forgot. It was another strange thing about Heaton Corners. It was so totally off the map that other than on a few computers in the school library, most people in Heaton Corners didn't use the Internet.

"Don't worry," she assured her friend. "We can look them up on my computer."

"Make the fangs sharper!" Stephanie said as Mary Beth drew a vampire in her notebook.

Ashley grinned as her friends started talking over one another, completely carried away by their excitement. She reached into her lunch bag and pulled out the apple that had been left at her locker. After rubbing the apple on her sleeve, Ashley took a big bite. It was just as delicious as it looked.

Then she glanced up and saw Joey walking across the cafeteria—walking right toward her—with a big smile on his face. The timing was no coincidence, Ashley realized. It was almost as if he'd been waiting to make sure she got the apple. She smiled back at him as he approached.

"Make the eye sockets bigger!" Danielle cried. "That skull should look really, really horrible and scary!"

Her timing couldn't have been worse, because at that very moment, Joey arrived at their table. The smile immediately faded from his face as he glanced at Mary Beth's notebook.

"What is this?" he asked in a low voice. "Is this for Halloween?"

None of the girls answered him. Ashley couldn't even look at him.

"What's the *matter* with you?" Joey asked. He didn't raise his voice, but there was a tone of revulsion in it that made Ashley shiver. "Why are you doing this? I already told you—"

"Why do you even care?" Ashley interrupted him as she dropped her half-eaten apple on the table. "What's wrong with this place?"

"Come on, Mary Beth," Joey said, almost pleading. "*You* know—I mean, at least your *mom* must know—"

Mary Beth looked at him like she had no idea what he was talking about, and Ashley was pretty sure she didn't.

Joey clenched the edge of the table with both hands and held on so tightly that his knuckles turned white. "Well, if you're going to be *stupid* about it, I'm going to— I'm going to have to—have to tell someone."

Mary Beth burst out laughing. "Really? Who are you going to tell, Chuckles? Are you going to tell your stepmommy?"

The other girls started to giggle—even Ashley. Joey gave her a long, hurt look before he turned and walked away. The sight of his shoulders, all slumped and defeated, made her wish she could follow him. She wished there was something she could say—or do—to make him feel better.

"Hey," she said, turning to Mary Beth and trying to change the subject. "Why did you call him Chuckles? Is that some kind of nickname?"

"Oh, Ash, the story is so funny," Danielle began.

"Ugh, no," Mary Beth said. "Please don't tell it right now. I will totally lose my appetite."

"Better eat fast, because I think Ashley deserves to know," Danielle replied.

"It's a good one," added Stephanie.

"Go on, tell me already," Ashley said impatiently.

"Back when we were in fourth grade, Joey's parents had a barn dance one winter," Danielle began. "The whole town was invited, and it was really nice—the barn was done up with all these twinkly lights, and there was a ton of food. . . ."

"Stew and dumplings and brown bread and, like, eight kinds of pie!" Stephanie chimed in.

"So for a while, at the start, all the kids were playing snow tag in the moonlight," Danielle continued. "It was really fun until we got too cold, so then we all went inside, and everybody was starving because we'd been running around in the snow, so we were all eating, and Joey was totally pigging out. And then Mr. Wagner got up and started telling jokes, and Joey started laughing really hard—"

"He was in the middle of a piece of pie," Stephanie remembered. "And he started to choke on it a little, and then—"

"He puked!" Danielle cried. "All over himself, with the whole entire town watching."

"Ugh," Mary Beth said, looking a little sick. "It was soooo gross."

"But also hilarious," Danielle added. "Because he'd

been eating so much, you know, and laughing so hard, and his big brother, Pete, yells, 'Whoa there, Chuckles!'"

"'Cause he upchucked," Stephanie explained. "And also 'cause he was laughing, I guess."

"Everybody called him Chuckles for the longest time," Mary Beth said. "People finally moved on last year, I guess."

"But a story like that will follow you around forever in Heaton Corners," Danielle said. "Honestly, they'll probably still be talking about it at his wedding someday."

Ashley tried to smile, but she didn't think the story was that funny. *Poor Joey,* she thought, sneaking a glance at him across the cafeteria. He was staring into space with such a deeply troubled expression on his face that she was filled with regret for laughing along with her friends.

It's not my fault, she thought. *Why is he so obsessed about us going trick-or-treating? He needs to chill out. It's just for fun.*

Ashley shoved the rest of the apple into her lunch bag. She wasn't hungry anymore.

CHAPTER 6

"Ugh—*oof*—there we go." Mrs. McDowell grunted as she used all her strength to shove open the barn door. "We really need to replace these hinges. This door barely opens!"

But Ashley had more important things on her mind. "Did you find it?" she asked eagerly.

"You bet I did," Mrs. McDowell replied as she dropped an enormous cardboard box at Ashley's feet. "Of course it was jammed into the very back of the attic, but I braved the spiders just for you."

"Yay! Thanks, Mom, you're the best!" Ashley cried as she opened up the box. Years and years of Halloween decorations were stored in it—everything she would need to get the barn ready for the spookiest Halloween party ever.

"More like *you're* the best," Mrs. McDowell replied, reaching out to ruffle Ashley's hair. "I can't believe you've spent your entire birthday cleaning out the barn."

Ashley shrugged. "It was no big deal. I just wanted to get everything ready for tonight."

"Well, it looks great in here," Mrs. McDowell replied, glancing from the freshly swept floor to the neatly stacked hay bales. "What can I do to help?"

"What time is it?"

Mrs. McDowell glanced at her watch. "Almost four. Dad's leaving to pick up the pizzas in about twenty minutes. Your friends are coming at six, right?"

"Right."

"That doesn't leave a lot of time for decorating and changing into your costume," Mrs. McDowell said, looking concerned.

"We're all going to put on our costumes together," Ashley said quickly. "So we can help each other get ready."

"Oh, okay," replied Mrs. McDowell. "Want some help with the decorating?"

"Sure," Ashley said. She knocked the box over so that plastic spiders, creepy masks, and fake tombstones spilled all over the barn floor. "Let's do it!"

By the time Ashley and Mrs. McDowell finished decorating the barn, it was completely transformed. Gauzy spiderwebs on the walls fluttered with the slightest breeze, and Ashley had used reams of tattered gray fabric to partition off a small circle in the middle of the barn. The fabric was so threadbare in parts that it looked like an ancient shroud. There were jack-o'-lanterns, each carved with a gruesome face, arranged against the walls. When Ashley turned on the battery-operated candles inside them, they flickered so unevenly that they cast spooky shadows over the entire barn. She shivered with delight as she realized that this barn was probably the spookiest place she'd ever been in her life—which made it the perfect setting for a Halloween sleepover party!

"Really outstanding, Pumpkin," Mrs. McDowell said as she looked around the barn. "I think your friends are going to love it! Now, are you sure you want to sleep out here?"

"Definitely," Ashley said.

"It might get pretty chilly."

"We can handle it," Ashley replied.

"Okay, well, if you change your mind, you can come in at any point. I'll leave the back door unlocked. And you know there's going to be a ton of scary movies on TV tonight. Might be fun to watch one really late. Just don't pick something too scary."

"Ahh! It's almost six!" Ashley said as she glanced at her phone. "Do you think Dad's back with the pizzas?"

"Probably," Mrs. McDowell said. "I'm pretty sure I heard the truck a few minutes ago. Let's get back to the house before your friends arrive."

When Ashley walked into the kitchen, the delicious smell of pizza was so strong that her mouth started to water.

"Hey, birthday girl!" Mr. McDowell called out. "I got *you* a special birthday surprise."

"What? What?" Ashley asked eagerly.

Mr. McDowell pointed to a plastic bag on the counter. "See for yourself!"

Ashley hurried across the room and peered into the bag. "Oh, awesome!" she said, laughing as she pulled out an economy-sized package of chocolate-covered marshmallow pumpkins. "My favorite! And now I have my own personal stash!"

Ding-dong!

"Somebody's here!" Ashley cried. She raced to the door and opened it to find Mary Beth—and her mother—waiting on the porch.

"Happy birthday!" Mary Beth and her mother said at the same time.

Ashley smiled back at them and said, "Thank you!" As she spoke, she noticed that Mrs. Medina was peering over her shoulder into the living room. Then Mrs. Medina craned her neck to look into the kitchen.

"Hi, Luisa," Mrs. McDowell called to Mrs. Medina from the kitchen. "Want to come in for a piece of pizza?"

"No thank you, Julia," Mrs. Medina replied. "I've got to get supper on myself."

Then, with a slight, satisfied nod of her head, Mrs. Medina gave Mary Beth a fast hug. "Have a good time, dear," she said. "Remember what we talked about. I'll pick you up tomorrow morning."

"Bye, Mom!" Mary Beth replied, giving her mother a kiss on the cheek.

"Bye, Mrs. Medina!" Ashley added. She watched as Mrs. Medina walked down the porch steps. Just as Ashley was about to close the door, Mrs. Medina turned around.

Oh no, Ashley thought. *She's going to talk to Mom. She's going to make sure we don't go trick-or-treating.*

But all Mrs. Medina did was bend down and pick up a package.

"Oooh! It's my birthday present from Maya!" Ashley exclaimed. She stepped into the twilight and grabbed the box that was wrapped in plain brown mailing paper with her name written on the top. She wasn't sure, but it felt like Mrs. Medina had been a little reluctant to let go of the package.

Ashley couldn't wait to open it. "She promised to send me something special."

"That's very nice. Have fun at your party tonight," Mrs. Medina said. Then she continued down the path to her car.

Ashley pulled Mary Beth into the house, and both girls dissolved into giggles. "Oh my gosh!" Ashley whispered. "I thought she was going to talk to my parents! I thought she was going to bust our party for sure!"

"She made me promise not to go trick-or-treating tonight, but whatever. I think she was looking for Halloween stuff," Mary Beth replied. "Like decorations and things. I'm sure she felt better when she saw that there weren't any, like, jack-o'-lights in your living room."

"Jack-o'-lanterns," Ashley corrected her. "And that's because they're all in the barn!"

Mary Beth's eyes lit up. "Really?"

"Oh yeah. Everything's all set up out there," Ashley said as she led Mary Beth into the kitchen.

"Hi, Mary Beth," Ashley's parents said.

"Don't worry, we'll get out of your hair," Mrs. McDowell continued. "But we do want to see you girls all dressed up in your costumes before you head out, okay?"

"Okay, okay," Ashley said, staring pointedly at the stairs. "See you later."

Mr. and Mrs. McDowell exchanged a smile as they left the kitchen.

"Look what my dad brought me—only the world's best candy! Want one?" Ashley asked Mary Beth.

"That's okay," Mary Beth said, shaking her head. "Maybe after pizza. But honestly, I don't like chocolate that much."

"What?" Ashley asked, pretending to be shocked. "Are you sick or something?"

Mary Beth grinned at her. "It's just not really my

thing. But sour gummies, on the other hand . . . if you have any of those, get out of my way!"

"I bet we'll get a lot of those tonight!" Ashley said, laughing as she ripped open the package. "I wonder what Maya sent. She said it was going to be something really special. . . ."

Mary Beth watched as Ashley opened the box. There, nestled in folds of tissue paper, was a necklace. As Ashley lifted it up, the shiny chain glinted in the light.

This is the amazing present? Ashley thought in confusion. Hanging from the chain was a familiar-looking pendant: shaped like a sideways figure eight, with a lump in the middle. Then, as Ashley took a closer look, she finally recognized the lump.

It was a snake's head, eating its own tail.

"I've seen that before!" Mary Beth said suddenly. "Like, here and there around town."

"Oh yeah. Maya told me all about it," Ashley replied. "It's a lemniscate—the symbol for infinity. Except it usually doesn't have this snake head. I guess, in this symbol, the whole lemniscate is a snake twisted around itself . . . devouring its own tail."

"Ugh," Mary Beth said, shivering. "Creepy."

"But perfect for Halloween," Ashley said. "And for my costume!"

"So when are you finally going to tell me what you're wearing?" Mary Beth asked.

But Ashley just smiled and shook her head. "It's a surprise. Don't worry, you'll find out soon," she promised.

Ding-dong!

"Really soon!" Ashley said as she and Mary Beth hurried off to answer the door. It was Danielle and Stephanie. The four friends chatted excitedly while they ate pizza in the kitchen. Then Ashley led them out to the barn. It took her four tries to get the door open, but that only helped to build the suspense. By the time it finally opened with an ear-splitting shriek, Ashley's friends were so full of nervous anticipation that they all screamed!

Ashley grinned as she thought, *I've never done Halloween with a bunch of newbies before. This is going to be awesome!*

"Okay, everybody," Ashley announced as they followed her through the gauzy curtains hung in the very middle of the barn. "Let's put on our costumes! And if you need any extra finishing touches . . ."

Ashley gestured to a bale of hay that was cluttered

with spooky masks, glow-in-the-dark hair spray, black lipstick, and a horribly realistic-looking bowl of fake blood that she had whipped up that morning.

"Look at all this stuff!" Danielle marveled.

"Help yourself!" Ashley said with a grin. "Remember, there's only one rule tonight: the scarier, the better!"

"Okay," Mary Beth announced as she grabbed a tube of jet-black eyeliner and some lipstick. "I need a spooky makeover. Somebody want to help me out here?"

"You got it!" Stephanie cried as she ran over. In a few minutes Mary Beth's gorgeous brown eyes were shadowed by thick, black lines that made her look much older. Her lips were stained with bloodred lipstick. There was fake blood dripping down the sides of her mouth and down her chin. She twirled around in a sleek black dress with draping bell sleeves. A black cape, lined with bloodred satin, completed her outfit.

"Mary Beth!" Ashley exclaimed. "You look amazing! Where did you get your costume?"

"Oh, I juth thewed it," Mary Beth replied. Then she frowned and pulled a pair of plastic fangs out of her mouth. "Sorry. I *sewed* it. It's hard to talk with these fang things in."

"Well, they're perfect. Totally realistic . . . for a vampire, that is," Ashley said, giggling. "Besides, you'll get used to the fangs after you've worn them for a little while. I was a vampire two years ago, and by the end of the night, I totally forgot I was even wearing them."

"I can't believe you sewed that whole thing so quickly." Danielle laughed. "I took the lazy way out. My mom's hot glue gun got the job done!"

The other girls turned to admire Danielle's costume. She was wearing black leggings and a form-fitting black hoodie that had been covered with bones made out of white felt. She was even wearing gloves with little white bones going down her fingers. She'd painted her face entirely white, except for gaping black holes painted around her eyes, nose, and mouth.

"I *love* it," Ashley said. "Can you do a creepy dance?"

"What? Like this?" Danielle asked as she started to dance in a corner of the barn. Against the darkness, only the bones on her costume were easily visible—making her look like a real skeleton.

"Okay. Guess who *I* am," Ashley said. She turned away for a moment, and when she turned around again, her friends screamed.

"Medusa!" they all yelled at the same time.

"Nice hair!" Danielle laughed, pointing at the snakes flowing down the back of Ashley's head. "Medusa is totally my favorite Greek monster."

"Right?" said Ashley, adjusting the toga she'd made out of an old sheet. "We learned all about her in English class last year. And when I found the shed snake skins, I knew I had to do something with them."

"Snake skins? What?" Danielle asked.

"These are real snake skins!" Ashley exclaimed, pointing to the brown and gnarled snake-shaped tendrils entwined through her hair. "I found them right here in the barn! When I couldn't find a place to buy a costume in town, I decided to dye them to look like live snakes and glue them to a headband. Genius, right?"

Mary Beth shrieked. "I *hate* snakes! I can't believe you put real *snakes* on your *head*!"

"Snake *skins*," Ashley corrected her. "And I'll do anything for a great costume." Then she turned toward Stephanie. "Hey, you've been really quiet. Let's see your costume. Time for the big reveal!"

There was a pause before Stephanie turned around. "What do you think?"

At first, Ashley wasn't sure what to say. Sure, Stephanie looked beautiful, all dressed up in a long white gown, with pretty makeup, sparkly jewelry, and a flowing veil on her head. But there was nothing scary about her costume—nothing at all.

Luckily, Danielle did the talking for her. "What are you wearing? You sister's old prom dress?" she asked bluntly.

"Yeah," Stephanie said. "I'm a bride."

"Um, we can *see* that," Danielle said in such a funny voice that everyone laughed. "But what's scary about it?"

Stephanie shrugged. "Nothing, I guess. Scary isn't really my thing."

"But, Stephanie," Mary Beth said, "we had a deal. We were all going to dress up as something scary, remember?"

"I didn't know that we *had* to do that," Stephanie said, looking away. "I'm sorry . . . I just . . . Does it matter?"

"I guess not," Ashley said.

"Well, I think it does!" said Mary Beth. "This is *Ashley's* party for *Ashley's* birthday and the only reason we even get to go trick-or-treating tonight is because of *Ashley*!"

"Okay," Stephanie relented quickly, turning to Ashley. "Help me be scary."

"Really?" Ashley asked. "You don't have to if you don't want to—"

"No, I do," Stephanie said. "Seriously. Now it's *my* turn for a scary makeover!"

Ashley put her hand by her mouth, frowning slightly as she examined Stephanie's costume. Then her whole face brightened. "I know what to do!"

Ashley perched Stephanie on the edge of a hay bale. "We don't even have to change your costume," she said as she applied white powder to Stephanie's face, neck, and arms, and added a smudge of purple eye shadow beneath Stephanie's eyes to create dark, creepy circles. Then Ashley coated Stephanie's hair with glow-in-the-dark hair spray before sprinkling more white powder all over her head. When Ashley was done, Stephanie's hair was entirely white, with the faintest hint of an otherworldly glow.

"Ta-da!" Ashley cried proudly. "Now you're a ghost bride!"

"I love it!" Stephanie exclaimed as she stared into a pocket mirror that Ashley had brought to the barn.

"You look spooky *and* pretty," Mary Beth told Stephanie.

"Wait a minute," Ashley said. "One last thing!"

She grabbed a red lip liner and drew a thin line across Stephanie's neck. A few drops of fake blood made the "wound" look even creepier.

"Now you're a *murdered* ghost bride!" Ashley announced. "My mom wants to be a total *mom* and take some pictures of us, so let's get that over with so we can get out there and trick-or-treat!"

The other girls followed Ashley back to her house where, to her surprise, her mom and dad were completely cool, taking only a couple of pictures before turning off their camera. "You have your cell phone, right, Pumpkin?" Mrs. McDowell asked. "And you'll remember to watch out for cars? And don't eat any unwrapped candy."

"Yes. Of course. Never," Ashley replied.

"Okay then . . . have fun," Mrs. McDowell said, opening the door for them. "And happy Halloween!"

The girls walked outside, where a full moon shone through a cloudless sky. The last of the autumn leaves rustled on the trees from a burst of cold wind; one plummeted through the night sky and got stuck in Mary Beth's hair.

"Whoops!" Ashley giggled. "Let me get that for you." As she leaned forward to pluck the leaf out of Mary Beth's hair, one of the snake skins brushed against Mary Beth's cheek. Mary Beth clapped a hand to her face, simultaneously jumping away and cringing in horror.

"Ahhhh! I'm scared already!" Mary Beth cried, but Ashley could tell from her tone that she was having fun.

"Just you wait," Ashley replied with a spooky smile. "It only gets worse from here!"

She had no way of knowing how true those words would be.

CHAPTER 7

"This way," Ashley said when they reached the road. "I think it's better if we follow Rural Route 13 toward town. The houses are closer together there, so we'll be able to hit more of them before we need to get back. My mom doesn't want us to stay out past nine."

"How come?" Stephanie asked. "There's nothing to be scared of, right? I mean, not really?"

"No, of course not," Ashley assured her. "It's just that that's usually when high school kids go out, and they can get kind of crazy. Like, throwing really stinky rotten eggs, stuff like that. Besides, by nine o'clock we'll have more candy than we can even carry!"

"I hope we get some chocolate peanut-butter bars," Stephanie replied. "They're my favorite."

As the girls continued down the road, a sticky, clammy mist surrounded them; every time Ashley moved her head, the now-wet snake skins flicked against her neck, sending shivers down her arms and back. The bluish light from the full moon made the girls cast elongated, distorted shadows that followed their every move. It was a perfect Halloween night, spooky in every way—almost too perfect.

"Do you see?" Ashley cried, pointing at Main Street.

"Trick-or-treaters!" Danielle replied.

"Hey, guys!" Mary Beth called out to them in her cheeriest voice. The two trick-or-treaters up the road didn't respond.

As the two groups came closer to each other, Ashley was a little shocked by how old-fashioned their costumes were—and how detailed. A red devil with razor-sharp horns approached them, carrying a carved pumpkin on a stick. His mouth moved up and down as though he was trying to say something, but only faint whispers were coming out. Ashley would have wondered about this if it weren't for her shock at the rest of his outfit. The grimace carved into the pumpkin looked so torturous that Ashley couldn't help but think that it took a lot of the fun out of Halloween. The clouds of sulfurous smoke that poured out of the pumpkin's eyes, nose, and mouth surrounded them, and Ashley and her friends started to cough, covering their mouths and noses.

The devil cackled at their discomfort as he danced in circles around them.

"What's wrong with you?" Ashley managed to sputter out just as the devil's companion, a small girl dressed as a bat, made her way into the haze, flapping her leathery—and very hairy—wings in Ashley's face. Ashley cried out when she caught a glimpse of the bat's face: the coarse brown hairs, the tiny piggish nose, the glinting gold eyes. It was the most realistic mask she'd ever seen.

"Mary Beth! Danielle! Stephanie!" Ashley screeched to her friends. She managed to lock hands with Mary Beth and Danielle, who had grabbed on to Stephanie, and the four girls started to run. Once they were safely away from the devil and bat, and Ashley was pretty sure they had moved on to torment other trick-or-treaters, she stopped running. She looked at her friends. Mary Beth and Danielle looked confused; Stephanie looked like she was about to cry. Ashley didn't know if that was from fear or from the acrid smoke.

"What was *that*?" Mary Beth asked, her voice high-pitched from fear.

"Okay, something like that has *never* happened to me before," Ashley said.

Stephanie didn't say anything, but from the way she looked longingly in the direction of her house, Ashley began to think trick-or-treating was going to get cut short.

"I promise that is *not* what trick-or-treating is about," Ashley assured her friends. "Those were just a couple of mean kids who think Halloween is an excuse to do whatever they want."

"Are we going to get sick?" Stephanie asked in a worried voice. "Do you think that smoke was, like, poisonous?"

"No way," Ashley said, shaking her head. "It smelled like a stink bomb, that's all." She pointed down Edgewood Lane. "Let's head down this street and start trick-or-treating."

Unsure of what to do, Stephanie looked at Mary Beth and Danielle. Danielle nodded.

Whew, Ashley thought, happy that trick-or-treating wasn't going to be a total bust.

"So, Ash, what do we do again?" asked Mary Beth. The lisp from her fangs was getting fainter each time she spoke.

She must be getting used to those fangs, Ashley thought, beginning to cheer up about the night that lay ahead of them.

Ashley grinned at her. "Watch and learn!"

The other girls followed Ashley up the front steps. "I'm going to ring the doorbell in a second," Ashley whispered to them. "When somebody opens the door, hold out your bag and yell, 'Trick or treat!' Then they'll put some candy in your bag and probably say something about how awesome our costumes are. And then we say thanks and go to the next house. Got it?"

"Got it," her friends replied.

"Okay! Here we go!" Ashley said, feeling that rare, once-a-year thrill of ringing the first doorbell on Halloween night.

Ding-dong!

All four girls held their breath, waiting expectantly for the door to open.

But nothing happened.

"I'll try again," Ashley whispered over her shoulder.

Ding-dong!

She cocked her head, trying to listen to any sounds within the house. Did she hear panicked whispering behind the door . . . or was it just her imagination?

Ashley hesitated for a moment. With all the lights on, she was almost positive that someone was home. But she thought it would be rude to ring the doorbell for a third time.

"Ashley . . ." Mary Beth whispered. "Should we maybe go? I think that—"

"What's that?" Danielle interrupted her, pointing a bony finger to the far corner of the porch.

Ashley turned to look and nodded her head in understanding. "Oh, that explains it," she told her friends. "Nobody's home after all, I guess. When people aren't home on Halloween night, they leave a bowl full of candy for the trick-or-treaters."

"How much can we take?" Stephanie asked as they approached the bowl, which was filled to the brim with candy.

"One or two pieces," Ashley told her. "Don't worry, we're going to get *plenty* of treats tonight! Come on, we can help ourselves."

But the moment the girls reached into the bowl, all

the lights outside—and inside—the house went out. They were plunged into sudden darkness!

"Ahhh!" Mary Beth and Stephanie cried.

"Aw, man. Now I can't even see what I'm getting!" complained Danielle.

With her hand in the bowl, Ashley could feel the crinkly foil and smooth plastic wrappers of the candy and her friends' cold fingers as they all grasped for a piece. "Do you guys want me to turn on my flashlight?" Ashley asked.

"I can see okay, with the full moon and all," Mary Beth replied.

The girls stuck some candy into their bags and hurried off the porch. "Well, that was kind of a letdown," said Ashley. "But I'm sure the next house will be better."

"Yes!" Stephanie suddenly cheered. "I got my favorite!" She ripped the wrapper and took a big bite of her chocolate peanut-butter bar—right in the middle of the street. Ashley started to crack up, relieved that her friend was starting to get into the spirit of things.

"What?" Stephanie asked with her mouth full. "I challenge you to find anything in the world that tastes better than chocolate and peanut butter. Don't even bother. You'd only be wasting your time."

"Come on," Ashley called out. "The porch light's on at this house."

With less trepidation than before, her friends charged right up onto the porch.

"Can I ring the bell this time?" Danielle asked.

"Of course!" replied Ashley.

Ding-dong!

But again, no one came to the door.

"Look," Mary Beth said, pointing at the porch railing. "Another bowl of candy."

Ashley shook her head. "Let's just grab some candy and try the next house."

Once again, when the girls reached into the bowl, the lights went out. This time, though, it was almost as if they expected it; nobody reacted at all.

"Maybe that's a Halloween tradition here?" Ashley asked her friends. "Or some kind of Heaton Corners–style prank?"

"Hey, who's that over there?" Stephanie asked as they neared the school. "And over there?"

"Over there, too," added Danielle, pointing across the street.

"Ha! I knew it!" Ashley cried triumphantly. "I *knew* there were lots of people who went trick-or-treating in Heaton Corners. Come on; let's go say hi."

"Maybe they'll know about some houses where people actually, like, come to the door," Danielle said.

I hope so, Ashley thought. She didn't want her friends' very first experience with trick-or-treating to be so totally lame . . . but that's how it was shaping up so far.

The school was dark, but by the light of the moon Ashley could see that the sidewalks outside of it were swarming with kids in costumes. There was an executioner, clad all in black with heavy metal chains clanking across his chest. His mask had just two thin slits for eyeholes. The sharp edge of his ax glinted in the moonlight; if Ashley didn't know better, she would've sworn it was real. There was a mangy dog, his hide bare and scabbed in places, who snarled at Ashley, and a tattered scarecrow who flopped down the street on limp and rubbery limbs. The smell of mildew was overwhelming as the scarecrow passed by, shedding moldy pieces of hay that swirled on the wind.

Ashley marveled at the extreme realism of all these costumes. On one hand, it was like her wish for only spooky Halloween costumes was being granted, but she didn't like it that she and her friends were outdone by every costume they saw.

She was starting to think that maybe there was a reason a lot of people in Heaton Corners ignored Halloween—it seemed like Halloween wasn't that much fun here. Only sinister.

Ashley and her friends walked over to a group of trick-or-treaters who were dressed as a witch, a werewolf, a zombie, and some sort of goblin with greenish skin and sharply pointed ears.

"Hey, you guys," Danielle called out in a jokey voice. "Identify yourselves!"

But the group of kids just stared at her.

She decided to try again. "It's us—Danielle Ramos the skeleton, Stephanie Gloucester the ghost bride, Mary Beth Medina the vampire, and Ashley McDowell, Medusa. Who's under these masks?"

The witch turned and looked at the school, as if she didn't really know what it was. The pause before she replied was just a little too long. "You don't know us," she finally croaked out in a whisper. "We don't go to school here."

Then the witch's hands, which must have been coated with some sort of wrinkle paste, fluttered up to the brim of her pointed hat. She knocked at it absently, dislodging a few cobwebs that fell to the ground. And . . . was that a real *spider* that hit the sidewalk? Ashley turned on her flashlight to get a better look, but it had already skittered away.

"Well, your costumes are amazing," Danielle added. "Ash, did you see this werewolf mask? It looks totally real!"

Ashley held up her flashlight and pointed it at the werewolf's face. Its wiry, tangled hair hung in a thick shag over tiny black eyes that glittered with a beady brightness; they were animalistic and yet so much more, as if some unexpected intelligence lurked just beneath the surface.

A terrible, snarling growl filled the air, making Ashley drop the flashlight at once. Then her friends started to giggle. "Totally realistic!" Danielle said approvingly. Next she turned to the zombie. "And you? The smell? *Yuck*, I have to give you props. That stink is serious. You really do smell like the undead! What did you do, roll around in a manure pile or something?"

As Mary Beth and Stephanie laughed nervously,

Ashley caught a whiff of the zombie, and suddenly she didn't think it was very funny. Where had she smelled it before, that sickly stench, almost sweetly repulsive, the middle stages of decay and decomposition? A little stronger, and she would've gagged.

Then the memory revealed itself to her: A few years ago, a mouse had died in the wall of their apartment building, and that smell—*that very smell*—had grown stronger and stronger, until the building manager had to come and put something in the wall to dissolve the dead mouse's body. It had been one of the creepiest things to ever happen in Ashley's life.

So far.

"Well, we should be going," Ashley said, trying to mask the panic in her voice.

"Hey, yeah, that reminds me," Danielle said. "So, have you guys gone to any good houses? Nobody's been answering the door for us."

"Well, tonight you can go anywhere," the goblin whispered suddenly. His voice was so quiet and so distant, Ashley could barely hear him. Then he turned his grotesque face up to the moon, as if to judge its position in the sky and figure out what time it was.

"Anywhere," echoed the witch. Then she reached for Stephanie's veil and twined the gauzy lace through her gnarled fingers. "Pretty," she said, and suddenly the witch's voice sounded very far away. "I always liked pretty things. Soft things."

"Have fun," Ashley said hurriedly, linking her arms through Mary Beth's and Stephanie's, hoping that Danielle would follow right behind them. "Hope you get a good haul."

"Bye, Stephanie," the witch called, waving . . . or reaching for her; Ashley couldn't tell which. "See you soon."

Ashley and her friends walked in silence for several blocks, more quickly than they had before, eager to get away from the crowd of trick-or-treaters at the school.

Then Danielle said what they all were thinking: "Freaks!"

And the friends broke into loud, contagious laughter, the kind that only comes from a place of fear.

"Probably some kids from Walthrop." Mary Beth sniffed. "Those losers should stay in their own town, huh?"

"Bet they came here just to play pranks," Ashley said wisely. "They didn't even seem to care about trick-or-treating." She caught Stephanie glancing over her shoulder again and gave her arm a quick squeeze. "Seriously, don't worry about those kids," Ashley said, trying to reassure her.

"I don't think they were kids," Stephanie said in such a soft voice that Mary Beth and Danielle didn't hear her. Her hand fluttered to her chest, then to her stomach, then clutched at the veil where the witch had held it.

"Are you—" Ashley began.

"Ash! Ash!" Mary Beth said in an urgent whisper. "You know who lives there, right?"

Ashley's gaze followed where Mary Beth's finger pointed. It was a handsome red farmhouse, with crisp white shutters bookending each window and a large porch that wrapped around the entire first floor. The house glowed with a golden, welcoming light; it seemed like the lights were on in every single room.

"Who?" Ashley whispered back—but in her heart, she was pretty sure she already knew.

"Joey!" Mary Beth replied. "Do you want to—"

Ashley cut her off. "I can't. Not with the way he feels about Halloween."

"Oh, come on!" Danielle goaded. "It's obvious he likes you, and you are obviously so into him."

And before Ashley knew it, Mary Beth and Danielle had dragged her up the front steps. "Good luck!" Danielle cried as she rang the Carmichaels' doorbell and ran away. Ashley would have followed them and fled the scene, unwilling to face Joey's wrath, except for the fact that the door immediately swung open and Ashley was face-to-face with Joey.

It was a face Ashley barely recognized. It wasn't just the lemniscates that had been painted on his cheeks with painstaking detail; even without looking closely, she could see the greenish glitter to the snakes' scales; the red drops of blood, falling as the snake devoured itself, that stood out so strangely against Joey's unusually pale skin. No, what really struck her was the horror in his eyes; they were an empty void of cold, black fear that made Ashley feel like her throat was closing up.

"Oh, Ashley," Joey whispered in a hoarse voice. "Please, please go home. And whatever you do, don't—"

"Noooooooooooooo!"

Joey and Ashley both jumped as a woman's voice

screamed. There were thundering footsteps racing down the stairs, followed by another scream.

"Noooooooooooooo!"

Then a woman Ashley assumed was Joey's stepmother appeared behind him. In one sudden motion, she yanked him away from the door and slammed it shut in Ashley's face.

Ashley heard the turning of a lock and hesitated for a moment as she listened to the loud sobs coming from behind the locked door.

Then all the lights went out.

For the first time in her life, Ashley was filled with genuine fear on Halloween night. Suddenly all the things she loved about Halloween—the costumes, the candy, the trick-or-treating—seemed trivial and foolish. None of it seemed that important anymore. And they sure weren't fun in Heaton Corners.

Somehow Ashley made it off the porch, back to her friends, whose faces were ashen.

"So that was . . ." she began. Then her voice trailed off.

"Yeah," Danielle said, and Ashley realized that she didn't need to say another word.

"Should we, um, go back?" Ashley asked. "Back to my house? I'm kind of not in the mood for any more trick-or—"

"Yeah," Danielle repeated.

And in the light of the full moon, glancing warily around them, the four friends started to run.

CHAPTER 8

No one said much on the way back to Ashley's house, but once they were in the barn, all the girls seemed to relax. The flickering jack-o'-lanterns, the wispy veils hanging from the rafters—they all helped Ashley start feeling deliciously scared—but not terrified—once more, which was precisely how she wanted to feel on Halloween.

"Let's check out our haul," Ashley suggested as she turned over her treat bag and dumped her candy on the floor. The other girls did the same.

"I can't believe we got so much candy!" Danielle exclaimed. "And that people just stick it out on their porch for us to take! That's crazy!"

Ashley just smiled at her. In reality, their candy haul was incredibly disappointing. Pathetic, even. They'd probably only gotten six or seven pieces each. *But they don't know how weak that is,* Ashley reminded herself. *They've never had Halloween before.*

"And we have birthday cake, too," Ashley said quickly. "And ice cream. And more candy in the house."

"So what do you want to do now, birthday girl?" Mary Beth asked. "I kind of don't want to take off my costume yet. I love wearing it!"

"Me too." Ashley laughed, twirling a snake skin around her finger as if it were a lock of her own hair. The other girls shrieked.

"Ooh, I know!" Ashley exclaimed. "Have you guys ever played Light as a Feather, Stiff as a Board?"

As she expected, the other girls looked at her blankly.

"It's a really spooky game that's perfect for sleepovers," Ashley continued.

"What do you do?" asked Mary Beth.

"So, one person lies down, and everyone else gathers around her, and you can actually make her *levitate,*" Ashley said. "It really works, too. I played it once in Atlanta, and my friend Rachel was totally floating, like, three inches off the ground!"

"That sounds awesome!" cried Danielle. "Let's do it!"

"Okay, who wants to go first?" Ashley asked. She turned to Stephanie, who'd been strangely quiet since they had returned to the barn. "How about you, Steph? You already look like a ghost."

"Sure," Stephanie said with a shrug. "Do I just lie down here? On the floor?"

"Yup," Ashley replied. Then she knelt down on one side of Stephanie. "Mary Beth and Danielle, you go take the other side."

When everyone was in position, Ashley dropped her voice to a hush. "Everyone put two fingers under Stephanie," she explained. "Now close your eyes. When I start saying 'light as a feather, stiff as a board,' you repeat after me, okay?"

Mary Beth and Danielle, their eyes already shut, nodded silently.

"And, Stephanie, don't move, not even a little bit. You've got to stay completely still," Ashley continued. "Everybody ready?"

Mary Beth and Danielle nodded again, but Stephanie didn't move.

Ashley slipped her index fingers under Stephanie's side, feeling the fine, soft lace at the end of Stephanie's veil. An image of the witch reaching for it flitted through her mind, but Ashley pushed it away as she closed her eyes. *Focus,* she told herself. *Focus.*

After several minutes of silence, during which Ashley could only hear her friends' quiet breathing, she started to speak, setting up the game. "Our friend Stephanie died today," she said in a low, somber voice. "Her heart stopped beating. Her blood stopped flowing. And we gather here tonight to say good-bye to our friend Stephanie, who died today. We gather around Stephanie's cold, lifeless body, which is *light as a feather, stiff as a board. Light as a feather, stiff as a board.*"

Mary Beth and Danielle joined in, their voices hushed and reverent. "Light as a feather, stiff as a board. Light as a feather, stiff as a board. Light as a feather, stiff as a board."

Light as a feather, stiff as a board.

After the girls repeated the chant several times, it happened.

Stephanie started to rise off the ground.

Light as a feather, stiff as a board.

It's working, Ashley thought as a thrill of apprehension tingled through her. *It's working!* Ashley felt no pressure from the weight of Stephanie's body; just the softness of her veil and the stiffness of her hair under that. Ashley did notice that her index fingers were freezing. *The barn floor is so cold,* she told herself before shoving the thought far from her mind. Ashley knew that she had to focus to keep Stephanie floating. If her concentration wavered, Stephanie would fall back to the floor, and the spell would be broken.

Light as a feather, stiff as a board.

Suddenly Ashley realized that she couldn't feel Stephanie's veil anymore.

She couldn't feel anything.

Ashley opened one eye and glanced up.

Stephanie was hovering five feet above her head!

Before she could begin to understand what had happened, or how, Ashley felt a surge of basic intuition: This was not right. She had never seen *anyone* hover so high during Light as a Feather, Stiff as a Board.

Mary Beth and Danielle, their eyes still closed, had no idea.

And still Stephanie continued to rise.

Without another thought, Ashley scrambled to her feet and lunged for Stephanie, who felt as light as a bird in her grasp. The spell was broken; Stephanie and Ashley both fell to the ground in a heap. Stephanie moaned.

"You okay?" Ashley asked. "Sorry about that."

"That was *amazing*!" Danielle cried, opening her eyes.

"Steph! You were levitating!" exclaimed Mary Beth. "How did it feel?"

"Really weird," Stephanie replied in a hollow voice. "I mean, I really felt like I was floating. Like I was completely weightless. Like I wasn't even here, actually."

"My turn," Danielle announced, lying down where Stephanie had been just moments before.

"Then me," said Mary Beth.

Ashley got up from where she and Stephanie were still lying, brushing the dirt and hay off her costume as she made her way over to Danielle and Mary Beth. As the seconds passed, she began to doubt whether she'd actually seen Stephanie floating. She didn't think she'd had a lot of candy, but now she was beginning to wonder, because she was clearly seeing things. Maybe this was all just the effect of too much sugar. But at the same time, she wasn't sure she wanted to play another round of Light as a Feather, Stiff as a Board.

"Coming, Stephanie?" Danielle asked. But there was no answer.

The three girls turned around to where Stephanie was lying just a second ago, but she wasn't there.

"Steph?" Ashley cried out. Still no answer.

Ashley got up and started searching the barn, but Stephanie was nowhere to be found.

"Could she have gone inside?" Ashley wondered aloud, running out of the barn.

As Ashley ran in the back door of her house, her parents glanced up at her from where they were sitting at the kitchen table.

"How's everything going, Pumpkin?" her father asked from behind his newspaper.

"Uh, great," Ashley replied. She felt bad lying to her parents. "Did Stephanie come in here, by any chance?"

"Not that we saw," said her mother. "And we've been sitting here the whole time. Why? Did she need a break from all the spookiness in the barn?"

"No, no reason," Ashley answered quickly. "We were playing a game, and I thought she might have come in here for something. She must be hiding somewhere in the barn. Bye, guys."

Ashley heard her parents wishing her a good time as she hurried out the door and back to the barn. She hated lying to her parents, but she didn't want to make them as alarmed as she was.

But when Ashley returned to Mary Beth and Danielle, she was surprised to see how calm they seemed to be about Stephanie's sudden disappearance.

"I bet I know where she went," Danielle said as she started eating a candy bar from her treat bag. "The last time the two of us had a sleepover, Stephanie totally left in the middle of the night. I didn't even realize she was gone until I woke up the next morning."

"That's weird," said Ashley.

"She absolutely does that, though," Mary Beth added. "She did it to me over the summer. When I talked to her the next day, she said she wasn't feeling well and she just needed to go home. I bet she's halfway there already. I wouldn't worry about her."

Ashley didn't know what to do. If she was still living in Atlanta, she would be totally freaking out right now, but it wasn't that late and it wasn't like Stephanie would get lost going to her house—Ashley lived a little farther out from the center of town than the rest of her friends, but not *that* far.

"If you say so," Ashley said, suddenly remembering

how well her three friends knew each other—and how little Ashley knew them.

"Want to play hide-and-seek?" suggested Mary Beth.

Ashley nodded, happy to focus on something other than Stephanie and where she had disappeared to, but she couldn't help thinking how hard her old friends in Atlanta would've laughed if someone had suggested that. Hide-and-seek was a game for little kids.

"You'll love playing hide-and-seek in a barn," Mary Beth replied. "It's really fun, especially at night, when there are so many shadowy places to hide."

"Just look out for spiders," Danielle joked.

"Home base will be inside the curtain. I'll be 'it,'" Mary Beth said. Then she shut her eyes. "One . . . two . . . three . . . four . . ."

Without making a sound, Danielle and Ashley slipped outside the curtains into the darkness of the barn. *Mary Beth was right,* Ashley realized as she glanced around. There were tons of great places to hide in the barn, from the stalls where horses and cows once lived to the hayloft high in the rafters.

"Eighteen . . . nineteen . . . twenty . . . twenty-one . . ."

Well, I guess the hayloft is out, Ashley thought as

Danielle dashed over to the rickety ladder and started to climb it.

"Forty-two . . . forty-three . . . forty-four . . ."

Yes! Ashley suddenly thought. *The wheelbarrow!*

On silent feet, Ashley crept across the barn to the back corner, where a bunch of corroded old tools were stored. Carefully, carefully, carefully she moved aside the hoe and the scythe and stepped over the saw. There was an old wheelbarrow behind all that junk that was big enough for Ashley to hide in. Its sides were coated with chipped red enamel, and the wheelbarrow was caked with mud and . . . and Ashley didn't want to know what else. Her muscles clenched as she climbed inside the wheelbarrow and crouched down behind it. In the darkness, Ashley grinned. It was a great hiding place!

"Ready or not, here I come!" Mary Beth called.

The only sound in the barn was Mary Beth's footsteps. Ashley strained her ears, trying to figure out where Mary Beth had decided to search first. It was so quiet.

Almost too quiet.

Bet she's looking in the stalls, Ashley thought suddenly. There were twelve stalls for livestock at the opposite end of the barn. If Mary Beth *was* looking in the stalls, Ashley could easily run to home base and be safe. But if Mary Beth was closer, Ashley knew she might get tagged.

It was a risk Ashley was willing to take. All her muscles tensed as she prepared to race across the barn. Then Ashley leaped over the side of the wheelbarrow and sprinted to the glowing circle in the center of the room. "Ollie-ollie-oxen-free!" she screamed at the top of her lungs, so caught up in the game she forgot to act cool about it.

"Aw, man! Where were you?" Mary Beth's voice echoed across the room.

"I'll never tell!" Ashley laughed.

Then Mary Beth poked her head through the curtains. "Come help me find Danielle."

Ashley shook her head. "No way! You're on your own," she replied.

"Oh, fine." Mary Beth sighed. "Be that way."

Ashley sat, all alone, in the center of the barn while she waited for Mary Beth to find Danielle. Mary Beth must have gone for stealth mode, because Ashley couldn't hear a sound.

After an interminable wait, Mary Beth's voice

echoed through the barn again. "I give up, Danielle!" she called. "You win. Come out, come out, wherever you are!"

But Danielle didn't respond.

"Danielle?" Ashley called. "Come out, okay?"

Still, there was no response.

"Danielle!" Mary Beth yelled, louder this time.

Ashley sighed in frustration as she got up. From what she knew of Danielle, it seemed like her to pull a stunt like this—to stay hiding long after the game was over, just to prove that she'd won. Ashley strode over to the hayloft, with Mary Beth following right behind her. Ashley pointed upward to indicate that Danielle was probably hiding there, and Mary Beth nodded her understanding.

"Danielle! I'm coming up," Ashley called. "You can't hide forever!"

Then she started climbing up the ladder. Ashley was halfway up when she felt the ladder start to shake; she looked down and saw that Mary Beth was climbing it too.

"Hang on," Ashley said. "I don't know how sturdy this thing is. We better just go up one at a time."

"Okay," Mary Beth said as she jumped off.

There was a tiny round window near the highest peak of the roof; bluish moonlight spilled through it, providing the only illumination in the hayloft. At first glance, Ashley couldn't see anything besides mounds of dusty, dried-out hay. Then she noticed a figure crouched in the corner.

Danielle, Ashley thought with relief. She hadn't even realized that she'd been holding her breath.

"You won, okay?" Ashley repeated as she walked across the hayloft, kicking up clouds of dust with every step she took. "Come on."

The figure didn't reply. It didn't even move.

"Hello? Earth to Danielle? Did you hear me?" Ashley said, unable to keep a note of annoyance out of her voice.

Still no response.

This is ridiculous, Ashley thought. She reached out and shook Danielle's shoulder.

Except it wasn't Danielle.

And Ashley didn't have a chance to figure out *what* it was.

Because the moment she touched the figure, its head fell off, and it rolled around the floor at her feet.

CHAPTER 9

The scream that escaped Ashley's throat burned like acid; she screamed so loud and so hard and so long that all the microscopic cells lining her throat turned red and raw like they'd been scraped with a grater. And yet she couldn't stop screaming, no matter how much it hurt.

"What happened? What happened?" Mary Beth yelled as she clambered up the ladder.

Ashley opened her mouth to reply, but all that came out was another scream.

"Ashley! Ashley!" Mary Beth shrieked as she started shaking Ashley's shoulders. "Ashley! It's okay! It's not Danielle! It's just a—look, *look,* Ashley, look at the floor, it's just a scarecrow!"

Ashley tried to understand what Mary Beth was

saying. She understood enough to stop screaming, at least. And when she looked at the ground, Ashley realized that it was a mannequin's head. Nothing but a piece of painted plastic.

"But I—I thought—I thought scarecrows were made of sacks and old clothes and stuff," Ashley tried to say. Her voice was hoarse.

"When Davis's Fine Fashions went out of business a few years ago, all the farmers bought their mannequins," Mary Beth explained. "They used them instead of the old kind of scarecrows. They worked great, too."

Yeah, Ashley thought, starting to blush in the darkness. *I bet they did, seeing as they're really incredibly scary.*

"So if that's not—" Ashley couldn't even say it. She swallowed hard instead and tried again. "So where's Danielle?"

Mary Beth shook her head. "I don't know. Are you sure she came up here?"

"Definitely," Ashley said.

"Well, then, let's find her," Mary Beth said with a quiet calm in her voice for which Ashley was enormously grateful.

"I must've seemed so ridiculous to you," Ashley said,

embarrassed. "Freaking out over a scarecrow."

"Nah," Mary Beth replied as she peeked behind a hay pile. "I hate those mannequins. They really give me the creeps . . . and I know all about them!"

Then a wide smile broke over Mary Beth's face, and she pointed at one of the hay piles at the other end of the loft. Ashley saw it, too: the toe of a shoe, peeking out just beyond the hay.

"She's been like this forever," Mary Beth whispered to Ashley. "Always has to find the best hiding place, always has to do everything a hundred and ten percent."

"There's always one like that," Ashley whispered back with a grin.

"Let's really scare her," Mary Beth replied. "Let's pretend like we're going back down into the barn, and then we'll sneak up on the hay pile and knock all the hay off of her."

"You got it!"

"I don't know, Ash, she must have gone back down after you hid," Mary Beth said loudly. "Because Danielle's definitely not up here."

"Sorry about that," Ashley said, just as loudly. "Let's look around downstairs some more."

Mary Beth held up her fingers one at a time, silently counting to five. Then both girls, yelling as loudly as they could, rushed at the hay pile. Their arms flailed around as they knocked the hay off the pile until, at last, they uncovered Danielle. She was sitting in the very middle of the hay pile, hiding in the small, uneven area by contorting her limbs in ways Ashley didn't think possible. "Ha! We *knew* it! We *knew* you were up here!" Ashley exclaimed.

"Ah. You, ah, you found me," Danielle said, her voice strangely flat. Then she straightened out her arms. *Crack! Crack! CRACK!* Ashley cringed at the sound of Danielle's bones groaning so loudly.

"I didn't know you were a gymnast," Ashley said as she reached out to help Danielle up.

"What do you mean?" Danielle asked.

"Well, it would take someone with superflexibility to position themselves the way you did to fit in that hay pile."

"Oh," Danielle replied, sounding distant. "I'm actually not very flexible. I wasn't even thinking about it."

"Did you hear Ashley freak out a second ago?" Mary Beth asked her old friend. "She discovered one of the mannequin scarecrows."

Danielle didn't bother to make eye contact as she stared ahead and mumbled a monotone, "No."

Ashley and Mary Beth exchanged a glance. "Maybe we should go inside for a bit," Mary Beth suggested. "It's getting a little cold out here."

Nobody spoke as, one by one, they climbed down the ladder from the hayloft and crossed the lawn to Ashley's house. The only sound was the cracking of Danielle's joints. Ashley certainly had heard knuckles and knees pop before, but nothing as constant and as loud as this. She began to wonder if maybe Danielle had hurt herself during hide-and-seek. What else could explain how this affliction had so suddenly come on?

As they entered the kitchen, Ashley gestured to the table where her parents had been sitting the last time she entered the house. "Why don't you sit down here?" Ashley suggested to Danielle.

Danielle shook her head and Ashley could swear she heard the bones in her neck cracking quietly beneath her skin.

"Are you in any pain?" Ashley asked.

"A little," said Danielle. "But I mostly feel weak—like my muscles aren't working."

"Okay, let me see what I can find for you up in the medicine cabinet," Ashley replied. "Stay right here. I'll be right back. Mary Beth, do you want to come with me?"

"Sure," Mary Beth replied. As the two girls headed out of the kitchen, Ashley could hear pops and cracks as Danielle managed to sit down in one of the kitchen chairs.

"What's wrong with her?" Mary Beth whispered, letting out a concerned sigh. "I didn't hear her fall or anything. It sounds like someone's playing the drums on her bones."

Or they're about to break, Ashley thought.

"I don't know, but there must be something we can do to help her," Ashley replied honestly, wondering if she should grab her mother. Her parents must have already gone up to their bedroom for the night as they were nowhere to be found downstairs. Ashley figured she didn't need to bother them just yet. "My mother always uses the hot water bottle when her muscles and joints are killing her."

"Ooh, my mom, too," added Mary Beth. "Good idea."

"I bet it's upstairs in the medicine cabinet," said Ashley. "Let's go."

As Ashley and Mary Beth were rummaging through the medicine cabinet in the upstairs bathroom, they heard a loud *crack!* from the kitchen. They thundered back down the stairs, and Ashley prayed that the noise hadn't woken her parents up. "Danielle!" she cried in an urgent whisper.

But when they reached the kitchen, it was empty. Danielle's chair sat in the middle of the room; her skeleton sweatshirt was draped across its seat.

"Danielle?" Ashley called in confusion. She turned to Mary Beth. "Is she in the bathroom?"

"I'll go check," Mary Beth replied. But she returned in moments, alone. "Not there. Not in the living room, either."

Ashley didn't say anything as she picked up Danielle's sweatshirt. She smoothed it on the table, noticing, for a moment, what a good job Danielle had done cutting out and gluing each white bone to the black shirt; how perfectly they fit together; how much it looked like a real skeleton.

"So, she just . . . left?" Ashley asked. "Without saying good-bye? In just her T-shirt?"

"I'm sorry, Ash," Mary Beth said quietly. "Maybe

she was feeling so bad that she wanted to be at home. Maybe she pulled a 'Stephanie.' I don't know."

"And what about that crack we heard?" Ashley wondered aloud.

"That was probably just the sound of the door slamming behind her," suggested Mary Beth.

"I don't understand. My mom would've driven her home," Ashley said. "Why would she just ditch my party like that? And Stephanie, too? Are they *mad* at me?"

"Mad about what? You didn't do anything," Mary Beth replied. "I'm just sorry they acted so weird. It's your birthday. That was so not cool of them."

Ashley gave Mary Beth a grateful smile.

"Besides, we will still have fun," Mary Beth promised. "What do you want to do now?"

Ashley shrugged. "Actually, if you want, we could watch a scary movie or something," she suggested.

"That's fine with me," Mary Beth said.

"I'll just go get our sleeping bags and stuff," Ashley said.

"I'll clean up in here," Mary Beth said, gesturing to some of the felt bones that had come unglued from Danielle's costume and now littered the kitchen floor.

"Oh, don't worry about it," said Ashley. "You don't have to."

"No, it's not a problem," Mary Beth replied. "Besides, it's your *birthday*. Cleaning up is the *last* thing you should do!"

Ashley laughed. "Okay, if you really don't mind. Thank you. I'll be back in, like, two seconds."

"You better," Mary Beth teased her. "Because there's still a ton of awesome fun stuff for us to do tonight."

As Ashley walked outside, she glanced over her shoulder. Through the window in the back door, she could see Mary Beth crouching on the floor, a bunch of foam bones in her hands. She immediately felt a surge of thankfulness for Mary Beth—for being so genuinely nice, so genuinely kind, for being such a good friend since the moment they'd met.

I'm lucky to know her, Ashley thought. *I'm lucky to have her as my friend.*

Then she turned away from the brightly lit kitchen and stepped further out into the night.

CHAPTER 10

When Ashley got back from the barn, lugging two sleeping bags, two duffel bags, and the rest of the candy from trick-or-treating, the kitchen floor was spotless—and Mary Beth was nowhere to be seen. For one awful moment, Ashley suddenly worried that Mary Beth had ditched her too.

"Ash? You back?"

A relieved smile spread across Ashley's face as she heard Mary Beth's voice. "Yeah," she called back.

"I'm in the basement," Mary Beth said.

Ashley kicked the sleeping bags down the basement stairs so that it would be easier to carry the duffel bags and candy.

"Did you get everything from the barn?"

"Um, I got our stuff," Ashley said. She didn't want to talk about the mess in the barn that she couldn't bear to clean up all by herself, or about how lonely it had felt to turn off every lamp in the jack-o'-lanterns and leave Stephanie's and Danielle's backpacks behind.

"I hope it's okay that I brought some snacks downstairs," Mary Beth continued.

"Of course it is." Ashley giggled. "I see you found the chips."

Mary Beth started laughing too. "I guess I have a salty tooth instead of a sweet tooth," she replied. "Is that even a thing? A salty tooth?"

"I have no idea," Ashley said, "but all I know is that means more candy for *me*!" She dumped the bags of candy on the table and started to rummage through the pile of treats.

"Hey," Mary Beth said, perking up. "Are those sour gummy worms?"

"Maybe," Ashley said slyly, raising an eyebrow at her. "But you wouldn't want those. You don't have a sweet tooth, remember?"

"For sour gummies, I do!" Mary Beth laughed. "Can I have them?"

"You got it," Ashley replied as she tossed the packet of candy across the room.

Mary Beth caught it with both hands and ripped it open. "Mmmm, they're the kind that have been dipped in sour sugar crystals!" she said as she pulled out a green-and-yellow striped gummy worm. "The best."

"It's weird you like those," Ashley replied. "They're really sweet."

"More sour than sweet, I think," Mary Beth said as she ripped the head off a gummy worm and began to chew. "Especially these ones. These ones are supersour. Ahhh, my mouth is all puckery! You want one?"

Ashley shook her head. "Nope. I just remembered I have those chocolate-dipped marshmallow pumpkins my dad gave me," she said. "I'll be right back."

When Ashley returned to the basement with her favorite candy, Mary Beth had finished the gummies and turned on the TV. "So, what do you want to watch?"

"A scary movie, for sure," Ashley replied.

"I've never seen a scary movie before," Mary Beth said, slouching into the corner of the couch. "Are they *really* scary?"

"Sometimes," Ashley said. "And sometimes they're

just ridiculous. Like, funny-ridiculous because the special effects are so bad or the plot is so stupid. Especially old scary movies can seem really silly today."

"It's funny how you know so much about scary stuff and I don't know, like, anything about it," Mary Beth said. "You must think I've lived some completely sheltered life or something."

Ashley wasn't quite sure what to say to that, so she grabbed the remote control and started flipping through the channels. *If Mary Beth has never seen a scary movie before, I don't want to traumatize her,* she thought. *Probably better to find something old and tame.* "Hey, this looks good," Ashley said out loud as she came across a black-and-white monster movie that had probably been made way before her parents were born. "What do you think?"

"Sure, whatever you want to watch," Mary Beth replied. "It's *your* birthday, after all!"

Ashley turned off the lights, and the girls sat next to each other on the couch, snacking on chips and making fun of the movie's ridiculous special effects. The monster costume, in particular, was hilarious—so much less believable than any of the costumes they'd seen on the trick-or-treaters that night. Ashley howled with laughter when the monster mask slipped so that she could see the actor's face beneath it.

After a while, though, Ashley realized that she was the only one cracking jokes. She sneaked a glance at Mary Beth, worried that her friend didn't like the movie and was just too polite to say anything. Mary Beth stared into the distance, unblinking. Ashley couldn't tell for sure, but it seemed like Mary Beth wasn't even looking at the TV.

"Hey," Ashley asked gently. "Do you want to watch something else?"

Mary Beth jumped a little, as if her mind had been miles away. "Oh, no, this is fine," she said, clearing her throat. "Actually, I'm really thirsty. Do you have anything to drink?"

"Oh, sure," Ashley replied, jumping up from the couch. "Sorry; I forgot about drinks. I'll be right back."

In the kitchen, Ashley dropped some ice cubes into two tall glasses. Then she opened a bottle of soda and filled each glass nearly to the brim. She walked slowly and carefully down the steps of the basement so that she wouldn't spill a single drop.

Mary Beth's eyes were filled with gratitude as she

took the soda from Ashley. "Thank you," she said before raising the glass to her lips and drinking greedily, finishing the entire soda in one gulp.

"Wow, you really were thirsty," Ashley remarked as she sat back down on the couch and sipped her own soda. The girls were quiet for a few moments as they watched the movie. Then Mary Beth cleared her throat again.

"Ash? I'm still thirsty."

"Here you go," Ashley replied, never taking her eyes off the TV as she pushed her own soda toward Mary Beth. "You can have some of mine."

But Mary Beth shook her head. "I don't want any more soda," she said. "I think it just made me thirstier."

"Oh. Okay," Ashley replied. "Hang on. I'll get something else."

Ashley brought Mary Beth's glass back to the kitchen, rinsed it in the sink, and filled it with cold, clear water. Then she brought it back down to the basement.

"Thanks so much, Ashley," Mary Beth said. But when she took a sip of the water, she made a face. Then she put the glass back on the table without drinking any more.

"Is something wrong?" Ashley asked.

"It just tastes . . . I don't know . . . bad," Mary Beth replied. She swallowed hard. "I'm still so thirsty, though."

"Um, well, we have orange juice, and milk," Ashley began, trying to remember what was in the fridge. "And apple cider, I think."

Mary Beth shook her head again. "I don't want any of that," she said, her voice cracking. "That all sounds awful."

"Well, sorry," Ashley said, stung. "I don't know what to tell you. Soda, juice, water, milk. That's what we have. What else would you want to drink?"

"I don't know," Mary Beth said.

Ashley tried not to sigh with annoyance. It had been a really long and lousy night. All she wanted to do now was watch some scary movies before she went to sleep. Why did Mary Beth have to start acting so high maintenance all of a sudden?

Then Mary Beth made a strange noise. Almost a whimper, almost a sob—it was unexpected enough that Ashley turned on the light so she could get a better look at her friend. Mary Beth's face was screwed up like she had started to cry, but her eyes were dry. No tears.

As Ashley's eyes adjusted to the light, she realized

that Mary Beth's skin was dry, too. And her lips. Her lips were so dry that they had cracked. Now they were speckled with tiny white shreds of flesh.

"Ashley, please," Mary Beth begged. "I'm so thirsty. Please. Please get me something to drink. I need something to drink."

"Of course," Ashley whispered, worried. She ran upstairs and poured glasses of milk and juice, then rushed them back to the basement. Liquid spilled out of the glasses all over the stairs, but Ashley didn't care.

"I brought everything we have," she said as she set the glasses on the table.

Mary Beth lunged for the juice, took a sip, and spat it on the floor. "This is terrible," she said, her voice tight and cracking. "It's spoiled or something."

Ashley reached for the glass and took a sip. "It tastes fine to me," she replied.

By this time Mary Beth had started pacing around the room. Her skin was deathly pale, growing whiter by the second. "I'm so thirsty," she said again. "I'm so thirsty. I can't—I can't swallow—"

"Here," Ashley said helplessly. "Try some more water."

"No. Terrible," Mary Beth snapped. Then she looked straight at Ashley with haunted, hollow eyes. "Ashley, what's happening to me?"

"I—I don't know."

As her anxiety increased, Mary Beth starting chewing on her cuticles as she paced. Suddenly, she cried out in pain.

"What? What happened?" Ashley exclaimed.

"I bit myself," Mary Beth replied. "My thumb. I'm bleeding."

Ashley laughed from sheer anxiety. "Next time take your fangs out *before* you start biting your nails."

"I did," Mary Beth replied. "I took them out hours ago."

As Ashley looked at Mary Beth, she noticed that a single drop of blood from her thumb glistened on her mouth.

Then Mary Beth licked her lips.

An instant peace, an enormous calm, flooded Mary Beth's face as she closed her eyes and smiled as if she'd just tasted the most delicious stuff in the world. She sighed with relief and brought her thumb to her mouth. Then she started sucking on it like she was a baby.

All right. Time to go, Ashley thought. Her eyes must have flicked toward the staircase, and Mary Beth must have noticed, because in one seamless motion, Mary Beth moved in front of the stairs, blocking them. She gave Ashley a thin smile; there was a smear of blood on her chin, real blood, not the fake stuff from earlier.

"Where are you going, Ashley? You don't have to go anywhere."

"I—"

"We have everything we need down here, right? Stuff to eat. Stuff to drink."

Was it Ashley's imagination, or was Mary Beth staring at her neck?

"Let's just hang out," Mary Beth continued. "Just sit down, okay?"

"Sure. Yeah. Of course we will. I just, um, have to go upstairs first," Ashley rambled. "Just for a second."

A flicker of annoyance crossed Mary Beth's face. "Come on, Ashley, what's the problem? It's not like I'm going to *bite* you. Sit down. *Sit.*"

Is there another way out of the basement? Ashley thought frantically.

There wasn't.

Ashley edged back toward the couch, never taking her eyes off Mary Beth, still dressed in her vampire costume, still sucking on her thumb. When Ashley finally perched on the edge of a cushion, Mary Beth smiled with relief. Ashley, her hand shaking, reached for the soda. She took a sip as Mary Beth approached the couch, licking her lips. Her dry, cracked, bloodstained lips.

Then Ashley threw the soda into Mary Beth's face.

As Mary Beth stood there, soaked and sputtering, Ashley shoved past her and ran up the stairs, two at a time, all the way to her mom and dad's bedroom. No slivers of light escaped around the closed door; her parents were probably asleep, Ashley knew, but she had to wake them up. Whatever was happening to Mary Beth was way too serious—and way too scary—for Ashley to handle on her own.

She tapped on the door, then knocked a little louder and pushed it open a crack. "Mom?" Ashley called in a soft voice. Then louder: "Mom? Mom?"

Mrs. McDowell sat up in bed. "Ashley?" she asked groggily. "Is everything okay?"

"Can you come downstairs?" Ashley said. "Mary Beth's not—she's not feeling well—"

"Of course," Mrs. McDowell replied, hurrying out of bed and grabbing her bathrobe. "Is she sick?"

"I don't know," Ashley replied. "She's just acting really weird. We were in the basement watching a movie, and then she—"

But Ashley couldn't finish her sentence. She followed her mom to the basement stairs, then suddenly thought, *I can't let her go down there!*

"Mom, wait!" Ashley exclaimed, grabbing her mother by the arm. "Never mind. Forget it."

Mrs. McDowell sighed. "Ashley, what's going on?"

"Nothing. I'm sorry I woke you up," Ashley continued. "Just—just don't go downstairs."

As soon as she'd finished her sentence, Ashley knew that she'd gone too far.

"Exactly *what* is going on down there?" Mrs. McDowell asked, pulling her arm free of Ashley's grasp. "Mary Beth? Can you come up, please?"

Okay, Ashley thought wildly. *That's better. There are more ways out of the house up here than down in the basement.*

But Mary Beth didn't appear. And she didn't answer, not even when Mrs. McDowell called her name again. Without another word, Mrs. McDowell marched downstairs. Ashley started to follow her but recoiled as she stepped in something wet and sticky. *Oh no,* she thought. *Oh no oh no oh no.*

She took a deep breath and clenched her fists so hard that her fingernails made pale little crescent moons in the flesh of her palms. Then she looked down and realized that she had stepped into a wet footprint.

The juice, Ashley realized. *I spilled it on the stairs. Mary Beth must have walked through it. . . .*

"Ashley? Is Mary Beth upstairs?" Mrs. McDowell called from the basement. "She's not down here. And where is everybody else? Stephanie and Danielle—"

"Hang on, Mom!"

Ashley crept across the kitchen floor, following a trail of moist, glistening footprints. They led straight to the back door, which was open just a crack, just enough to let in the night air so that a damp chill filled the entire kitchen. Ashley shivered and hugged herself, but she knew that her goose bumps didn't come from the cold air. They came from what she saw on the doorknob.

A smear of bright-red blood, still wet, dripping, even. Someone who was bleeding—someone with a bleeding thumb, perhaps—had rushed from this house, rushed through this door so quickly that she hadn't even stopped to close it. And in that chilling instance, Ashley realized that Mary Beth was gone. Her three new friends—the three girls who had made the move to Heaton Corners bearable—had all walked out on her birthday party, without even saying good-bye.

"Ashley! Did you hear me?"

Ashley turned around to see her mom standing in the doorway. "What?"

"I asked where everybody is?" Mrs. McDowell repeated.

Ashley shrugged and looked away. She didn't want her mom to see that her eyes had filled with tears. "I don't know. They left. I guess."

"They left?" Mrs. McDowell asked incredulously. "In the middle of the night?"

"Well, Stephanie and Danielle left earlier," Ashley said. "And I guess—I guess Mary Beth decided to leave too."

Mrs. McDowell gave Ashley a look—the one with the raised eyebrows, the one that said *I think there's something you're not telling me*—but Ashley didn't care.

"Did you girls have a fight?" Mrs. McDowell finally asked.

"No," Ashley said. "I have no idea what happened! They didn't even say good-bye. None of them did."

Then it happened: A single tear spilled down her cheek. Ashley wiped it away with the back of her hand, angry at herself for crying.

Mrs. McDowell sighed. "I would've driven them home! I can't imagine what got into Mary Beth to leave like that. She didn't need to walk home all by herself at night. I've got to call her parents."

"Mom, no," Ashley said. "Please. You can't do that."

"Ashley, I have to," Mrs. McDowell replied. "If it were you, I'd want someone to call me."

"Please, please don't," Ashley begged. "Do I have to spell it out for you? They all walked out of my birthday party. If you call their parents, you're only going to make it worse. Please, Mom, please don't call them."

Mrs. McDowell gave Ashley a long look while she tried to decide what to do. Then she sighed. "Okay, Pumpkin, I won't," Mrs. McDowell finally said. "I'm sorry. Sometimes I forget how tough middle school can be. This must be a really disappointing birthday for you."

"Yeah. You could say that," Ashley replied in a soft voice.

Mrs. McDowell walked across the kitchen and gave her a big hug. "Why don't you go to bed now, Ash?" she asked. "It won't seem so bad in the morning."

Yeah, right, Ashley thought to herself, but all she said was, "Okay. I just have to go back down to the basement for a sec."

"Good night, Pumpkin," Mrs. McDowell said as she gave Ashley another kiss. "Happy birthday. Next year will be better."

It can hardly be worse, Ashley thought as she tried to smile at her mom. Then she slipped into the basement, where she ripped off her Medusa costume and threw it in the trash. The only thing she kept was the lemniscate necklace; it was a present from Maya, which made it special.

Next Ashley gathered up all the Halloween candy so that she could throw it away too. Ashley didn't want any reminders of the worst night of her life. But just before she dumped it all in the garbage, Ashley saw a simple chocolate bar and thought, *Why not?*

She ripped off the wrapper and ate it in two bites. It tasted stale and waxy; not even worth the effort of chewing. Ashley swallowed hard, on the verge of tears again, as she trudged upstairs to her bedroom. No matter how much she tried to focus on something else—on *anything* else—all she could think of was the way her friends had walked out on her birthday party, leaving Ashley all by herself on what should've been the best night of the year.

It was the meanest trick anyone had ever played on her in her whole life.

CHAPTER 11

Ashley was used to the disappointment of November first, a day marked by sleepiness and a steady, deflating realization that the fun of Halloween *and* her birthday was over for another full year. The sugar crash didn't help, either. But this year, November first really was the worst. It was the longest, loneliest day, a day during which Ashley wished, constantly, that her friends would call. Or text. Or stop by. Or do *anything* to explain their behavior the night before—to reassure her that it was all just a joke. That they still wanted to be her friends. The more Ashley thought about that scene in the basement with Mary Beth, the more she started to doubt her own memories. It made no *sense* that Mary Beth would start acting crazy like that. And the soda—Ashley nearly groaned when she remembered *throwing a soda* in her best friend's face. No wonder Mary Beth had stalked out of her party without even saying good-bye. Ashley desperately wanted to apologize . . . if Mary Beth would ever speak to her again. When she hadn't heard from anyone by late afternoon, she finally mustered up to courage to call them, but there was no answer at the Medina, Gloucester, or Ramos households.

The thought of Monday morning, of seeing them at school, was almost unbearable. What would she say? Would she just pretend like none of it had happened? What if—Ashley could hardly bear to think of it—what if they completely ignored her?

That's me, she thought bitterly. *The outcast of Heaton Corners.*

And by Sunday night, when an entire day had passed without any contact from Mary Beth or Stephanie or Danielle, Ashley was sure that that would be the case.

She walked to school on Monday with a persistent heaviness in her chest, a combination of panic and dread that made it a little harder than usual to breathe. She found herself dawdling along Perseverance Creek, as if she could somehow delay the inevitable by walking just a little more slowly than usual. The only thing that happened, though, was that the loud brass bell started ringing while Ashley was still a block away from school. She broke into a run and was a sweaty, disheveled mess by the time she tore into homeroom—long after the bell had stopped ringing.

Mr. Thomas barely looked up as Ashley raced into the classroom. "No announcements today," he said quietly as he scanned the front page of the newspaper.

Ashley breathed a sigh of relief when she realized that she'd dodged getting a demerit for being late. At least *something* was going right today.

Only then did she notice the empty desk to her left.

Wait a minute, she thought. *Where's Mary Beth?*

Then everything started to make sense. *She must be home sick,* Ashley realized. *She was probably getting sick on Saturday. That's why she was so thirsty. Maybe she had a fever or something. Maybe* that's *why she was acting so strange. I bet it was the smoke from that pumpkin. That's what made everyone feel so sick.*

For the first time since Saturday night, Ashley felt a stirring of hope. It lasted all the way until second period, when she realized that Stephanie and Danielle weren't at school, either, and the teacher made no mention of them being out sick. They were just not there. No one else even seemed to notice. And by third period, the desks where Stephanie, Danielle, and Mary Beth would've sat in history class—the one class that all four girls shared—had been removed.

"Mr. Thomas?" Ashley asked as she approached the teacher's desk after class.

"Yes, Ashley?" He was reading the newspaper again and didn't even bother to look at her.

"Um, I was wondering . . ."

"Speak up, Ashley."

"Do you know where Mary Beth and Danielle and Stephanie are?"

The newspaper crinkled as Mr. Thomas turned the page. "They moved away over the weekend."

"What? That's impossible," Ashley replied, and Mr. Thomas looked up at last. He gave her a sharp glance, a warning.

"Sorry, sir," she said quickly. "But I don't understand—"

"The life of a farmer is a hard one, Ashley," Mr. Thomas interrupted her. "Many families find they just don't have what it takes. And with winter on the horizon, they were wise to leave now. Before it got any worse."

At that point, he snapped the paper so forcefully that Ashley knew their conversation was over. "Thank you, sir," she murmured and ducked out of the classroom.

Ashley had minded her manners as best she could, but she didn't believe for one minute that *all* three of her friends and their families had moved away on Sunday, so suddenly and without any warning.

When the McDowells had moved to Heaton Corners, Ashley had known about it for months beforehand. It had taken weeks just to make all the arrangements!

And Mr. Thomas's explanation made no sense. *The Medinas have lived in Heaton Corners forever,* Ashley thought. *If anybody can handle farm life, it's them.*

The conversation with Mr. Thomas left Ashley with more questions than answers. But no one at school seemed to have the answers—and if they did, they weren't willing to share them with her.

The first thing Ashley saw when she got home was a large box on the porch. She recognized Maya's handwriting immediately and ripped open the box before she even went into the house.

There was another box inside it, and inside that box, Ashley found the most beautiful pair of boots she'd ever seen. Knee-high, made of soft brown leather, they were really and truly grown-up boots. If it had been any other day, she would have imagined how amazing they'd look with her brown corduroy skirt or her best pair of jeans. But not today.

There was a card, too.

Happy birthday, little sister! Just because you're a farm girl now doesn't mean you can't have a decent pair of boots. Just promise me you won't wear them to do chores or shovel manure or anything disgusting like that. These boots deserve better. Wish I could help you celebrate your special day. Is Mom making a doughnut cake?

Love, Maya

P.S. I really hope this package gets there in time for your birthday! If it's late, don't blame me, blame my midterms!

Ashley was closing the boots back up in their box when she realized something.

The *boots* were the awesome present Maya had promised to send her.

Not the lemniscate necklace.

An uncomfortable prickling crawled along the back of Ashley's neck as she realized something: The package with the lemniscate had no address on it. It was never mailed. There were so many questions whirling around her mind that Ashley couldn't think straight.

Who left me the necklace?

Where are my friends?

What happened to them?

And, of course, the biggest question, the one that had haunted her since she had arrived in Heaton Corners and seen her first snake lemniscate and watched grown women freak out over a cake with spooky decorations and stumbled into the secret room in the corner store: *What are they hiding here?*

Ashley wasn't sure how she would find the answers.

But she was determined to try.

She walked around to the barn for her bike, doing her best to ignore the leftover Halloween decorations she still hadn't cleaned up. Then Ashley started pedaling as fast as she could.

Stephanie lived closest to her, in a dark-blue two-story house that had a cramped, pinched feel to it. From the outside, it looked the same as it had the one time Ashley had hung out there . . . except for the FOR SALE sign out front, swinging on squeaky hinges as a chilly breeze ushered in dusk. A flare of disappointment surged through Ashley; maybe Mr. Thomas was right. Maybe her friends *had* moved away.

Then Ashley got the strangest sense that someone was watching her. She turned around, half expecting to see Stephanie walking up behind her. . . .

But no one was there.

The same thing happened at Danielle's house . . . or, rather, at what used to be Danielle's house, because it was very clear to Ashley that no one lived there now. The windows stared at her blankly, like empty eyes that had lapsed out of focus. Somehow Ashley found the courage to peek into one of the windows. Some of the chairs had been knocked over; there were clothes and papers strewn across the floor. Ashley couldn't shake the feeling that Danielle's family had left in a hurry.

And she still couldn't shake the feeling that she was being watched.

Or maybe that she was being *followed*.

It was quickly getting dark, but Ashley climbed back onto her bike, determined to stop by the Medinas' house before night fell. The Medinas owned the largest ranch in Heaton Corners, which was good, considering Mary Beth had five little brothers and sisters. It was a beautiful homestead, with rolling acres of green pasture and not one but two gray barns to house their cattle and sheep. Mary Beth had promised Ashley that she could come over and play with the baby lambs in the springtime, but as Ashley walked up to the ranch, she knew that would never happen. Already the property had a deserted air about it; there was a loneliness that had settled over it like a cloud of dust. Ashley's intuition tugged at her, and something deep inside said, *Go away, go away, go away from here.*

But Ashley pressed on, determined to find out what had really happened to Mary Beth.

She owed her that much, at least.

There weren't any trucks in the long, circular driveway that swooped in front of the house, and a heavy padlock dangled uselessly from the gate. Right away Ashley knew that that was wrong. The animals could escape if the fence wasn't kept locked.

They could've escaped, at least, if they'd still been there. But it took only one peek in each barn—which were also unlocked—for Ashley to realize that not a single living being was left on the Medina ranch.

She had to check the house, though. She couldn't leave without checking the house. The creak of her footsteps across the porch was deafening; it seemed possible that the whole town could hear her. It was harder than Ashley expected to peer in the windows when every part of her pulsed with fear, when all her instincts told her to flee.

But she did it anyway. She looked in the windows. From what she could see, the Medina house was in perfect order, with everything in its proper place, except for the kitchen, where the table was still cluttered with yesterday's breakfast dishes. Soggy pieces of half-eaten toast, crusty egg yolks, cold bacon studded with congealed grease, two happy flies buzzing around it all. That's when Ashley really knew, without a doubt, that the Medinas were gone. Mrs. Medina would never leave the breakfast dishes on the table like that.

So that was that. It was obvious now; Ashley couldn't deny it anymore. Mary Beth was gone, and so was Danielle, and so was Stephanie.

Right?

Then something caught her eye around the corner of the house, a faint flicker that appeared and disappeared so quickly that Ashley couldn't be sure she'd seen anything at all.

Then she heard the cracking, the popping, like someone walking over dead branches but louder, deeper: a skeletal crunch.

And then she heard the voice.

Ashhhhhhhleeeeeeey . . .

Ashhhhhhhleeeeeeey . . .

A whisper that she could not only hear but also feel, a tickling breath in her ear, a raspy hiss across her neck.

Ashley was certain then that she was not, in fact, alone.

She stumbled off the porch, blinded by terror, jumped on her bike, rode away all wobbly, almost unable to keep her balance. She rode and she rode and she rode, but she didn't go home, and she didn't stop until she somehow remembered the way to the red farmhouse. There wasn't any candy on the porch this time, but there were lights on inside. Ashley couldn't seem to catch her breath; she held on to the porch railing as her lungs clenched and her heart thudded unevenly; she forced herself to take long, slow, deep breaths. The smell of fallen apples filled the air, sweet and cider-y and tinged with decay. It was a comforting and familiar smell, especially when mixed with the scents of damp leaves and the woodsmoke that was drifting from the chimney.

Ashley didn't know what would happen when she rang the doorbell. But she had to believe that Joey would talk to her. That Joey would tell her what he knew, even though he had pointedly ignored her at school all day, going out of his way, it seemed, to avoid her.

Because if he didn't, Ashley didn't know who would.

Her finger was surprisingly steady as she reached for the doorbell.

Ding-dong.

Moments later the door swung open. Just like on Halloween, Joey stood in the doorway, but this time his face was free of lemniscates and his eyes were free of fear. There was a quiet resignation in them, a simple sadness that made Ashley want to curl up in a ball and cry.

"Hey, Ashley," Joey said.

She opened her mouth, but no words came out.

"I guess you want to talk, right?" he asked. "You want to sit down?"

Ashley nodded and let Joey guide her over to the porch swing. His arm brushed against hers when he sat next to her, and the swing rocked back and forth, back and forth, as the last pink light of sunset washed over them. How many times had Ashley imagined hanging out with Joey, just the two of them?

But not like this.

Never imagining something like this in a million years.

She found her voice. "My friends," she said awkwardly. "Do you—do you know what happened to them?"

Joey was silent, and for an awful moment Ashley thought, *He won't tell me, he won't, he's just like everybody else in this horrible town,* and so she started babbling, "Please, Joey, I have to know, because I'm afraid something bad—like something *really* bad—happened, and I can't bear—"

"Hey, hey, slow down," Joey said gently. He reached

for her hand and held it tightly in his own. "When my stepmother started uncovering the truth about Heaton Corners, she made me promise not to tell anyone, for fear we'd be run out of town." Joey took a deep breath. "But I guess that doesn't matter much anymore now that everyone sees what the curse can do."

Ashley nodded, eager for information.

"I don't know that much," Joey said. "But I'll tell you everything that I *do* know, okay?"

Ashley continued to nod.

"Heaton Corners is cursed," Joey began.

Cursed? Ashley thought. *Cursed?!* But she forced herself to remain quiet as Joey continued talking.

"It's an old curse. Something terrible happened here a long time ago—so terrible that nobody talks about it, just like nobody talks about the curse. They just go about their whole lives pretending it doesn't exist. And so they've forgotten what the real danger of Halloween is in Heaton Corners. But there are a few people who think silence is more dangerous than the curse itself. And those people told my stepmother all they know. And there were many people, like my aunt, Mary Beth's mother, who didn't want my mother telling them anything unpleasant, anything they didn't want to hear."

"But what *is* the danger?" Ashley asked. "I mean, what *kind* of curse?"

Joey shook his head. "It has something to do with Halloween. Something about trick-or-treating. Mary Beth's mother never let her go trick-or-treating because of the scary kids who roam the streets. She thought they were the curse of Heaton Corners on Halloween night. But they aren't the real danger. Kids who go trick-or-treating in this town disappear . . . and are never seen again, except on Halloween night."

Ashley covered her mouth with her hands. *You did this to them,* she told herself. *It's all your fault.*

"You guys didn't know," Joey said, as if he could read her thoughts.

"But I went trick-or-treating," Ashley said, the sudden realization crashing over her along with a wave of nausea. "Is something—is something going to happen to me?"

"Well, not now," Joey replied. "At least, I don't think so. The curse takes effect pretty fast, I think. Before midnight on Halloween."

"So why was I spared?" Ashley asked. "Why me? Why not them?"

"I don't know," Joey said simply. "I think the lemniscate might have helped."

Ashley gave him a sharp look.

"The necklace," he explained. "I saw you wearing it on Halloween. I was so glad. I was afraid maybe you wouldn't."

The realization that dawned on Ashley burned slow and bright. "Wait—so you—were you the one who—"

"Yeah. I left the necklace on your porch," Joey said. "It's one of the things my stepmother believes in—a talisman that wards off the curse."

Ashley didn't want to ask her next question, but she had to. "But what about the other girls? Why didn't you give one to them too? You knew that we were *all* going trick-or-treating."

Joey gave her a crooked smile. "I did," he replied. "I think their parents intercepted them. The people in town who work so hard to ignore the curse *hate* the lemniscate. Because when other people see it, they start asking questions."

Ashley remembered, then, the look on Mrs. Medina's

face when she spotted the lemniscate painted on the mailbox post. "So the one on the post—"

"Yeah. That was me too," he admitted. "I just always wanted you to be safe. From the moment I saw you, the first day you came to school."

"Thank you," Ashley whispered, but she wished more than anything that Joey hadn't tried so hard to protect her. She didn't deserve to be protected—of that, Ashley was certain. Not after she'd put her best friends in such danger. There was nothing Ashley could do or say that would change the truth: If only she'd never begged them to trick-or-treat with her; if only she'd never invited them to her birthday party; if only she'd never moved to Heaton Corners, her friends would still be safe.

The burden of that knowledge was liable to crush her.

Ashley jumped off the swing and started pacing back and forth. "No," she said. "No. No. I don't accept that there's nothing we can do. There has to be something, Joey. A curse? What does that even mean? No, there has to be something. There has to be someone—"

Ashley stopped abruptly. Then she turned around and ran off the porch.

"Ashley!" Joey yelled. "Wait! Where are you going?"

"There *is* someone, Joey!" she yelled as she raced down the road, and in her haste, forgetting her bike. "There is someone who knows more than me . . . and more than you . . . more than your stepmother." Then she disappeared into the twilight.

"Hang on!" Joey called as he ran after her. "I'm coming with you!"

CHAPTER 12

Miss Bernice was just locking up the Heaton Corners Grocery and Dry Goods when Ashley and Joey arrived, sweaty and red-faced from running. She didn't seem surprised to see Ashley.

"Was wondering when you'd turn up," Miss Bernice said. "Expected you yesterday, to be frank."

"You know," Ashley said, pressing a hand over her chest as she tried to catch her breath. "You know what happened to them."

Then Miss Bernice sighed and reached for Ashley with a gnarled hand. Ashley tried not to flinch as Miss Bernice patted her shoulder. The old woman's touch was strong and steady.

"Not your fault, dearie." She sighed. "Not really. The

fault goes back a long way, back before your grandparents were even born. Why don't you come inside for a bit? Settle yourself before you go home?"

Miss Bernice unlocked the door to the store. Ashley and Joey exchanged a glance before they followed her inside. The black cats looked up from their food bowl, startled by Miss Bernice's unexpected reappearance.

"You have to tell me what happened to them," Ashley said. "I know you know. I know it."

"Why do you think that?" Miss Bernice asked as she reached down to pet her cats.

"Well, that room," Ashley said. "With all the names! And the lemniscate on the door! And you warned me. None of the other adults in this town warned me, but you did."

Miss Bernice didn't say anything.

"Please," Ashley said, and her voice wavered on the brink of tears. "Please. I have to help them. I have to get them back."

Miss Bernice sighed heavily as she rose to her feet. Then she shuffled off to the bathroom, where the cleaning supplies were kept, and opened up the secret room. To Ashley's horror, she saw three new, crisp white slips of paper with the following names written on them: *Mary Beth Medina, Danielle Ramos, Stephanie Gloucester.* To see their names written out like that only strengthened Ashley's resolve to save them. If she could.

"I keep this room so they won't be forgotten," Miss Bernice said. "This whole town is set up for forgetting. But I think these unfortunate kids deserve better than that."

"Miss Bernice," Joey spoke up. "Can you tell us about the curse?"

There was a long silence. "I can't," Miss Bernice said. As she turned away, despair surged through Ashley; she'd been so sure that Miss Bernice, at least, could help—

"I'm afraid it takes too much out of me these days," Miss Bernice continued, her voice muffled as she rummaged in a small cupboard. "But read this, and if you have any questions, I'll do my best to answer them."

Miss Bernice dropped a slender book in Ashley's hands, then shuffled out of the room. Ashley and Joey huddled close together as Ashley opened the burgundy leather cover. She didn't realize that she was holding her breath as she read the first page.

October 31, 1957

My name is Bernice Jackson.

I write this chronicle on the twenty-fifth anniversary. It is based on the stories that Chester Matthews told me, in secret, late at night, when no one was listening.

At least, I don't think anyone was listening.

Chester is gone; he couldn't bear to mark another anniversary. He does not write to me. To anyone. He said, before he left, that one way or another, he was never coming back.

I believe him.

And so I think it is acceptable for me to break my promise and commit this account to paper, so that it would not be lost with Chester, or if anything should happen to me.

I hope that Chester will forgive me.

But more than that, I hope he will forgive himself.

Ashley paused and glanced at Joey out of the corner of her eye to make sure he had finished reading the first page before she turned it.

From the whiteness of his face, she could tell that he had.

1931 was a hard year for most places. Not even Heaton Corners was spared. Two years of bad weather left more ruined farms—and ruined families—than the community had ever seen before. And yet they pulled together, best as they could. Most of them. After all, neighbors helping neighbors is the Heaton Corners way.

But not everyone suffered during the lean times. Charlotte Snowden was a lucky one. Her father's fortunes only increased, amid all the suffering, and she lorded it over the other children, some of them going to bed hungry at night, and Charlotte stuffing herself with anything that her heart desired. It wasn't right and it wasn't fair. But that didn't matter then, and it hardly matters now. When Halloween came around, the children cobbled together their costumes out of scraps and cast-offs. Nothing fancy, no, not for the children of Heaton Corners. Except Charlotte, of course. Her parents hired an honest-to-goodness dressmaker to fashion her whatever she wanted. That's the way Charlotte lived, and Chester says she wasn't even grateful for it. She just acted as though the whole world owed it to her. And so the dressmaker sewed for Charlotte a glorious snake-charmer costume, with a green shimmering skirt stitched with golden thread. There were more gold bangles on her arms than you could even count, and earrings made with real rubies. They even special ordered a rubber snake in a basket, for Charlotte wanted to put on a big show in her father's barn. All the children were invited and it didn't matter if they wanted to attend or not; their parents commanded them. That's how much power the Snowdens had. Charlotte bragged for weeks, until the other children were so consumed with jealousy that they could no longer tell right from wrong. At least, that's what Chester said. I suspect he is too hard on himself. He was only a child. They all were.

And so it was decided, among the children, that it was time for Charlotte to be taught a lesson. A little bit of comeuppance after how she'd rubbed their faces in her fortunes. So on Halloween night, out back behind the Snowdens' barn, somebody—Chester never would tell me who—swapped the rubber snake for a real one. Charlotte started her snake-charmer dance, and then she reached into the basket and pulled out a real snake. She started screaming, and all the kids laughed and laughed and laughed at Charlotte.

They'd waited a long time to see her get what she deserved.

But what they didn't know was that the snake was poisonous, and it had bitten Charlotte on the thumb. Her screams weren't from fear, they were from pain. But nobody realized that until Charlotte dropped to the ground, twitching and shuddering with pink foam bubbling out of her mouth, and then she went quiet and still. So quiet and still . . . because Charlotte was dead.

Ashley turned to Joey. "That's the Halloween tragedy?" she asked, her voice hardly louder than a whisper.

Joey slowly shook his head. "I think . . . I think that's just the start."

Ashley didn't want to keep reading. She did. She didn't.

She didn't have a choice.

Of course the children were horrified by what had happened.

They were severely punished. Even now, twenty-six years later, Chester couldn't speak of it without all the

color draining from his face, his skin the color of chalk. After all the punishments, after all the remorse, there would have been forgiveness, though, especially in a town like Heaton Corners.

But sometimes the dead don't forgive.

It's not right to speak ill of the dead. However, by all accounts, Charlotte was small and mean-spirited in life.

Death only magnified those qualities, transforming them into a toxic swill that poisoned her spirit.

Chester believes, really and truly believes, that Charlotte's spirit spent the next year scheming so as she could enact revenge from beyond the grave that would be so gruesome, Heaton Corners would never recover.

Halloween Night, 1932. The town wanted to forget what had happened to Charlotte. The children carried on with their festivities as they'd always done, dressing up as scary monsters and attempting to have a little fun in a year that somehow was even worse than the last. Then, after the trick or treat, that's when it all went so wrong.

One by one, the children started eating their

candy—the very candy that their families and friends and neighbors had given them—and then the fits started.

In her haste to turn the page, Ashley accidentally tore it, just a little . . . but she didn't even notice.

Chester, the lone witness; Chester, the lone survivor; Chester, the diabetic boy who every year watched his friends with longing as they devoured their Halloween candy. Chester, spared by a quirk of physical infirmity. He never could speak of all that he saw as the children were transformed into monsters, though I coaxed and coaxed—told him he was safe now—begged him, really, to share what he knew.

And now he is gone, and he is never coming back, and so here I am, left to bear my guilt alone for what I did, twenty years after these events, a new girl in this old town, making friends with children who were too young to remember; too young to know. I miss you, Cecily. I miss you, Sarah. I am so sorry. Can you ever forgive me?

I'll never leave you. I promise. I will be here for all

the days of my life, and I promise I will find a way to bring you back.

That was the end of the account; Miss Bernice hadn't written another word. As if she somehow knew that Ashley and Joey had finished reading, she slipped back into the secret room without making a sound.

"So, I'm confused," Joey said before Ashley could ask the question pressing down on her heart. "What happens to the kids? When they disappear?"

"They don't disappear," Ashley corrected him. "They turn into their costumes."

"You're both right," Miss Bernice replied. "After they consume the candy and the curse takes a hold of them, they disappear. And they only reappear once a year, on Halloween night, forever doomed to be the actual monster their costume had represented. But, you know, what I think is that they're never very far away. Right now, even, they might be all around us."

Ashley remembered the odd trick-or-treaters they'd encountered in front of the school—the witch and the werewolf and the zombie and the goblin—and felt like crying.

"But you kept your promise, right?" Ashley blurted out. "You found a way to undo the curse?"

Miss Bernice's lips were so pale that they seemed invisible against her ashen face. "I never should have made that promise. There was never any way to keep it."

"But how can that be?" cried Ashley. "It's been, like, eighty years! Surely *someone* found a way—"

"If only." Miss Bernice sighed. "Would you be standing here now if they had? The people tried everything to get their children back. There was a desperate ritual for some years. . . . On Halloween night, the parents would round up all the snakes they could and twist them into the symbol for infinity, partly as an offering to Charlotte's spirit and partly as a plea for forgiveness."

"So that's where the snake lemniscate comes from," Joey said.

"Well, it's all a bunch of bunk." Miss Bernice sniffed. "The lemniscate is more useful for identifying who knows about the curse than it is for warding it off."

"You're wrong," Ashley said, louder than she meant to. "Because I went trick-or-treating and I ate some candy and look at me. I'm fine."

"Oh, dearie," Miss Bernice said, giving Ashley

a smile full of pity. "Of course *you're* fine. You weren't born in Heaton Corners. Didn't I mention that? It's only the children who were born here who are in danger. I should know. I moved here when I was twelve years old. Convinced all my new friends to sneak out and trick-or-treat with me."

Miss Bernice turned to the wall and grazed her hand across two of the slips of paper, very yellowed and nearly crumbling with age. *After all these years,* Ashley thought, *she still misses them. She still feels responsible.*

It was, for Ashley, like peering into a crystal ball and glimpsing a future from which there was no escape. *But there must be,* she thought desperately. *I can't live with this shadow hanging over me for the rest of my life.*

"I don't get it," Joey said suddenly. "How come nobody *knows* about this? How come nobody *talks* about it? If Mary Beth and Stephanie and Danielle had known . . ."

"It was a bad decision," Miss Bernice said. "There was a town council meeting in the late 1940s that lasted into the wee small hours of the morning. And by the end of it, everyone so fraught and exhausted, so many despairing parents, a vote was taken by secret ballot, and it was decided that the curse should never be spoken of. There were economic concerns, you see. If word got out, who would want to live here? Who would want to buy the food we grow? It was decided that the curse must be kept secret for the town's survival. And what happened? People forgot. Sure, Halloween wasn't practiced anymore, but people forgot why. They figured they wanted to keep their living children safe from the monsters who roamed the streets, but they didn't know the real and horrific danger was that there was a chance their children could turn *into* those monsters."

"Where are their families?" Ashley asked. "I went by their houses—"

"I assume they were forced to leave," Miss Bernice replied matter-of-factly. "After all, the townspeople wouldn't want a scene.

"Makes it all the more heartbreaking on Halloween night—the plight of the lost children, I mean. They always go to familiar places, when they can remember how to get there," Miss Bernice continued. "Home and school especially. That's why the townspeople started putting candy on their porches. It's the last way they have to show the children that they're loved. Still. Always. After all.

"Of course, they're not really children anymore." Miss Bernice brought her voice down to a hush. "And they get more vicious as the night wears on. Quite nasty they can be, especially if someone forgets the candy. The Petersons learned that the hard way. Skipped the candy bowl one year—and that night their house was burned to the ground."

"So there's nothing I can do?" Ashley asked. "There's nothing I can do to help my friends? Nothing I can do to . . . to *save* them?"

She held her breath while she waited for Miss Bernice's answer. The rest of Ashley's life hinged on it—whether all the years to come would be tainted with the memory of what had happened to her friends, or whether she could somehow redeem herself and somehow make amends for the worst thing she'd ever done.

"No. Nothing."

Ashley turned away then, so consumed by her shame and guilt that she couldn't bear for anyone to see her. She wanted to run away to some deserted place so that she'd never have to face anyone ever again.

"Wait, dearie."

Miss Bernice knew, of course, exactly what she was going through.

"There is one thing."

Ashley spun around, her eyes—her entire face—bright with hope.

"On Halloween night, you can try to reach them," Miss Bernice said. "To remind them of their humanity. To show them that they haven't been forgotten. If you're brave enough, of course. It won't be easy. And it won't be safe. But I always felt . . . well . . . it's the least I can do."

There was a long silence.

"Can I just—have a minute in here?" Ashley finally asked. "By myself?"

"Whatever you want, dearie," Miss Bernice replied. "This room will always be open to you." She guided Joey out the door and gently closed it behind them.

Ashley looked from wall to wall, from name to name; she was surrounded. There was too much to register, at least in one night, but Ashley knew that was okay. She'd have plenty of time to get to know each one.

Besides, right now, there was something very important she had to do.

The names of Mary Beth, Danielle, and Stephanie

were lined up in a row, three friends who would never be parted. She brought up images of her friends in her mind. The freckles across Danielle's nose. The dimple in Stephanie's chin. And the kindness in Mary Beth's eyes. She reached up and touched each name in turn, just as she'd seen Miss Bernice do.

"Whatever it takes," she whispered to their names. "Whatever it takes. I'll be here for you. Forever."

She whispered because she wasn't alone; Ashley was sure of it. And then she felt it; someone's fingers snaking through her hair.

Missssssss you, Ashhhhhhhleeeeeeeey.

Missssssss you.

EPILOGUE

She was polishing her necklace with the edge of her shawl, not that it did much good; the necklace was old now, tarnished with age and wear, but she still liked to shine it up when she had a spare minute. It was a comfort to feel the familiar, serpentine curves in her hands, to hold something that had stayed the same even though so much had changed.

She was polishing her necklace, just to pass the time, when the little bells above the door tinkled. She looked up and saw the girls, so young, so giddy, so unaware, and her heart sank.

How many times, she thought sadly. *How many times must I bear witness?*

"The chocolate ones!" one of the girls giggled.

"Sugar-crystal sticks!" cried another.

"Wait a minute." The third laughed. "You don't need to buy a bunch of candy. The whole *point* is that other people *give* it to you!"

"But I don't want to wait!" replied the first girl. "Trick-or-treating doesn't happen until nighttime, right? And it's still an hour until sunset."

"Okay, fine." Her friend sighed. "Just get a little, though. Believe me, you're going to have a candy stash that will last for weeks!"

"No," the old woman said.

Either they ignored her, or they didn't hear her. The old woman didn't care.

"No," she said again, louder. And then louder still: "No! Trick-or-treating is forbidden here! You cannot do it! You cannot do it!"

The three girls exchanged a glance, right in front of the old woman, as if she couldn't see the mockery in their eyes.

"I beg you," she continued. "You can't imagine the danger. Go home! Go home to your parents and stay inside today!"

"Okay! Okay, Mrs. Carmichael! Don't get upset,"

one of the girls said quickly. She put her candy back on the shelf and gestured for her friends to do the same. "Don't worry, okay? We'll be fine."

Then she shot her friends a look, and they hurried out the door without another word.

The old woman followed them to the door as fast as she could, but in truth she wasn't very fast anymore. *That was stupid,* she scolded herself. *You should've waited. If they'd gotten the candy, they would've used the ScanPad to buy it, and you'd have their names and addresses. You could've told their parents—*

But it was too late now.

She could just see them in the distance, all golden with youth and promise, shining with the light of the setting sun. For two of them, their last day was almost over.

For the third? Well, she'd find her way back to the store.

They always did.

The old woman hobbled back to the secret room. She had to make some space on the walls, space for the new names she'd be adding in the morning.

They'd needed to expand the secret room some

years ago, but somehow she and her husband just didn't have the heart to do it.

It was always the same: A decade would pass without needing to add more names. That led them to hope, against all their better judgment, that their warnings had gotten through to everyone in the town—that everyone remembered the real reason why you couldn't go trick-or-treating in this town and that another child would not fall victim to the curse.

Eventually, though, those hopes were always dashed.

When she'd shuffled the papers around enough to accommodate the new names, the old woman decided that she might as well close up early. There was still so much she had to do when she got home. Find the extra blankets—it was going to be a cold night, and a long one, and at her age she really shouldn't take a chill. Fill the bowl with their favorite candy—of course she hadn't forgotten, not even after all these years. And, of course, the metal neckband.

The ghost and the skeleton weren't much of a worry. They could howl and scratch at her as much as they wanted; she didn't really mind. It was nothing compared to what they'd endured these past seventy years. But her neck, on the other hand. That needed protecting. Vampires just can't help themselves.

She wasn't scared; not too scared, anyway. In fact, she was looking forward to seeing them again.

Ashley always did like to spend her birthday with friends.

DO NOT FEAR—
WE HAVE ANOTHER CREEPY TALE FOR YOU!

CONTINUE READING FOR A SNEAK PEEK AT

You're invited to a

CREEPOVER™

It's All Downhill from Here

"So, exactly how far away from home is this place?" asked Maggie Kim, as she slouched down in the backseat of her parents' car. She ran her fingers through her dark, shoulder-length hair.

"Just a little more than four hours," Maggie's mother replied cheerfully from the front passenger seat.

"Might as well be four days," Maggie mumbled to her best friend, Sophie Weiss, who sat in the backseat beside her.

Sophie smiled, trying to make Maggie feel better. Her soft freckled face beamed out from under a mop of thick, curly red hair. She was taller than Maggie, despite the fact that they were the same age. In fact, their birthdays were just a couple of weeks apart.

Maggie and Sophie were seventh grade classmates in a big middle school in a suburb of Denver, Colorado. The two were inseparable, and so when Maggie learned that she had to make the trek to the mountains for the long weekend, she invited Sophie along. After all, a sleepover with her best friend was better than being stuck in a strange house with only her family all weekend. She wondered how many sleepovers she and Sophie would have left together, if her parents' crazy plan went through.

"As long as the skiing rocks, I don't care how far away it is," said Maggie's older brother, Simon. Simon was captain of his high school ski team.

"That's not a surprise to anyone, Simon." Maggie replied. "You spend every weekend on the slopes."

"I can't believe there aren't any ski resorts up on this mountain already, Mrs. Kim," Sophie said.

"That's why this would be the perfect investment, Sophie," Mr. Kim chimed in from behind the wheel.

"A perfect investment in *boredom*," Maggie quipped. "We'll be like a million miles from civilization. Not to mention all my friends." She reached around Sophie's shoulder and gave her a hug.

"What friends?" Simon teased.

"Shut up," Maggie shot back. "All you care about is that this place has mountains and snow. You don't care about people."

"Sure I do, Mags," Simon said. "People have to make the skis, and run the lifts, and—"

"You'll be able to visit your friends on the weekends, honey," Mrs. Kim interrupted, knowing that the current backseat conversation could only move in one direction—escalation into full-fledged sibling warfare.

"I've managed somebody else's hotel for years," Mr. Kim pointed out.

"And done a fantastic job at it too," Mrs. Kim added.

"Thank you, dear. And your mother has been the maitre d' at some of the finest restaurants in Colorado. We've always dreamed of starting our own hotel. So when the Wharton Mansion was posted for sale yesterday, and for such a steal, it seemed like the perfect opportunity to realize our dream. It really sounds just right from the description the realtor gave us when we grabbed the keys from her office this morning," Mr. Kim said.

"She told us that the previous owner of the house, 'Old Man Wharton', died about a year ago," Mrs. Kim continued. "No one has even been inside the house since then, because of a battle over the will. They finally settled the estate two days ago, and so she posted the listing before she had even seen or cleaned the place."

"We'll be the first ones to see it!" Mr. Kim said enthusiastically.

"Lucky us," Maggie moaned. "So does this place have any neighbors? What, like five miles away?"

"No!" Mr. Kim cried, as if Maggie had just said the most ridiculous thing in the world. "More like three."

"Oh, that's a lot better," Maggie said sarcastically.

"I'll come visit," Sophie said. "After all, BFFs are BFFs."

"I know," Maggie said. "But you'll get to go home. To a real town. With real people. I'll be living full time up in the middle of nowhere with real bears."

Mrs. Kim turned to face Maggie. "I wish you'd give this a chance. This is very important to us. At least take look at it before you decide it's going to be a nightmare."

"Fine," Maggie said under breath. *A living nightmare, the perfect description for this. The only thing missing is zombies.*

The last leg of the trip passed in complete silence until Maggie felt the car slow down. "Are we here?" she asked.

"Almost," Mr. Kim said. "We're in the closest town.

It's called Piney Hill, population 300." Maggie sat up and looked outside. Most of the buildings were shuttered, or were dark and closed for the night.

"Wait. This is the town?" Maggie cried in disbelief.

"Just five more miles up this hill and we're there!" he said, his excitement growing.

Slipping and sliding a bit on the icy hill, the car finally made it to a long twisting driveway. Ahead Maggie spotted a sprawling mansion. She couldn't believe her eyes.

"It's just what they call a 'fixer-upper,'" Mr. Kim said enthusiastically, anticipating everyone's reaction.

"It should be called a tear-it-downer!" Maggie exclaimed.

"Now Maggie. I—"

"Wait," Maggie interrupted, pointing to one of the windows on the first floor.

Through the heavy snow she could just make out the face of an old man. He was staring down at the driveway, glaring directly at their car. The light from the room he was in illuminated his whole appearance, making him look unnaturally bright.

"There's someone already in the house!" Maggie cried.

WANT MORE CREEPINESS?

Then you're in luck, because P. J. Night has some more scares for you and your friends!

Who's There?

In Heaton Corners, there are scares, mysteries, and surprises around every corner, especially on Halloween night! Fill in the spaces on the grid according to the list below to discover another spooky sight. The space that corresponds to 6A is already filled in for you. Can you fill out the rest of the grid? Watch out!

7A	2G	14B	1L	5F	11G	3G	6R
5B	7H	2J	15H	14M	4N	12O	7R
12B	2I	16D	8L	4G	12A	14O	10R
4C	6B	8J	16F	15M	15N	5P	16J
2E	16E	2D	10L	2H	6E	12F	11R
5E	10A	9J	14C	16M	12H	6P	6A
8A	13G	1K	17L	9A	16N	12G	5G
13E	4I	12E	1M	11H	13F	9P	14N
4F	14H	8K	7K	17M	4O	10P	7F
6G	13I	9I	2M	5H	5I	14F	3C
3H	4B	10K	11P	2N	6O	12P	7G
2F	14I	6F	3M	11A	15G	10J	13H
7P	8R	15C	16I	3N	8O	13P	9R
14G	4H	13Q	4M	13B	16H	5Q	8P
6H	11F	17K	16G	12R	10O	11K	

READY TO SOLVE?

WE DARE YOU!

	1	2	3	4	5	6	7	8	9	10	11	12	13	14	15	16	17
A																	
B																	
C																	
D																	
E																	
F																	
G																	
H																	
I																	
J																	
K																	
L																	
M																	
N																	
O																	
P																	
Q																	
R																	

YOU'RE INVITED TO . . .
CREATE YOUR OWN SCARY STORY!

Do you want to turn your sleepover into a creepover? Telling a spooky story is a great way to set the mood. P. J. Night has written a few sentences to get you started. Fill in the rest of the story on the lines provided and have fun scaring your friends.

You can also collaborate with your friends on this story by taking turns. Have everyone at your sleepover sit in a circle. Pick one person to start. She will add a sentence or two to the story, cover what she wrote with a piece of paper, leaving only the last word or phrase visible, and then pass the story to the next girl. Once everyone has taken a turn, read the scary story you created together aloud!

Last Halloween was the scariest night of my life! Zombies, witches, and ghosts wandered the streets, jack-o'-lanterns grimaced at me around every corner, and haunted sounds followed me and my friends as we trick-or-treated. But things started to get really strange when my friends and I ended up in front of the old house at the end of my block. We weren't even sure anyone lived there, but when we rang the bell, the door creaked open. We came face-to-face with . . .

THE END

A lifelong night owl, **P. J. NIGHT** often works furiously into the wee hours of the morning, writing down spooky tales and dreaming up new stories of the supernatural and otherworldly. Although P. J.'s whereabouts are unknown at this time, we suspect the author lives in a drafty old mansion where the floorboards creak when no one is there and the flickering candlelight creates shadows that creep along the walls. We truly wish we could tell you more, but we've been sworn to keep P. J.'s identity a secret . . . and it's a secret we will take to our graves!